VALUE BEYOND VISUALS

By: Joseph Provine Jr.

There is value beyond every visual that you face in life.

Acknowledgements

To my father: Dad, my bold, assertive Father and prophetic minister, you raised me and trained me to become a bold man of God. You never changed or switched up on me. You filled me up with gas when I almost went to E and you continued to push me through my adversities until I pressed past them. Back in 1st grade when I struggled writing, you helped bring me out of that by making me overcome that disability and now because of that I was able to write this book. I truly do thank you from the bottom of my heart. Love you exceedingly.

To my mother: To the virtuous queen in my life whom I submit to. Honestly, you've done so much for me so where do I begin? You've had so many responsibilities to take care of but somehow you managed to take care of all of them seemingly with so much ease and grace. You never let anything take away your loving kindness instilled in you by the Lord and extended that to me throughout my whole life. And I can truly sincerely say that you are a pure virtuous woman of God. And that alone in itself is rare. Whenever I read the thirty-first proverb, I think of you every time. Love you with all of me.

Mom and Dad, thank you all both for showing me the true love of Christ. Love, Love, Love you all.

Table of Contents

CHAPTER 1: GROWING UP

"Don't be like your father!" "Don't be like your father!" "DO! NOT! BE! LIKE! YOUR! FATHER!" These were the words spoken to me by my mom growing up. It wasn't easy being born in my situation, much less growing up in it for over eighteen years. My dad, as you would guess, was far from perfect. Mama would always tell me how those who exalted themselves would be humbled and those who humbled themselves would be exalted. According to Mama, my biological dad was "one of those" who exalted themselves instead of being humble. "Marlin, make sure you keep yourself humble now. You don't wanna' end up like ya' deadbeat Daddy." She'd say to me.

I never knew my biological dad growing up. I've seen pictures of him hugging Mama or staring into the camera with emotionless expressions on his face, but on a personal level, I never knew him. Mama would always tell me that he was arrogant. She told me he always ignored her precautions and warnings when it came to pursuing the street life. Ironically, in the hoods of Chicago, where we were currently living in, was dangerous. So, I could never understand why Mama was so disgusted by the influence that the streets had on him.

To be specific, my dad was charged with possessing illegal drugs with the intent to distribute them along with two counts of resisting arrest because of his belief that he was innocent while possessing the drugs. Unfortunately, because of this, the court sentenced him to serve time in the county jail. Initially, he was sentenced to ten years for the combined charges, but more misfortune followed him even after him serving just a couple years.

My dad, while serving only his fifth year in jail when I was only five years old, got involved in a brawl with some of the other inmates.

Consequently, the court charged him with second degree murder. This led to him being transferred to a prison and given another fifteen plus years on top of the five that he initially had left to serve. I vaguely remember visiting him on the few occasions at the county jail when I was younger. I remember sitting behind a glass window staring at a semi teary-eyed man who despite being teary-eyed remained nonchalant.

This would always confuse me in the few times that I remember seeing him. How could someone who is supposed to be my dad have no emotion for me or Ma? Mama would often tell me how the bad decisions that he made were the cause of us being in the bad position that we were in. She spoke about how she'd constantly warn him of the dangers of dabbling in the street life. But more importantly, she'd mainly talk about his refusal to listen because of his verbal commitments to stay loyal to his "hustle" and "crew" leading him to his downhill. My twelve-year-old sister Julia and I figured that the words "hustle" and "crew" were associated with negative avocations such as selling drugs and gangs, but we never exactly knew what the terms "hustle" and "crew" referenced. I knew that Mama knew what they meant, and she would never tell us the exact meaning when we asked, but I always had this sense that the terms had a meaning that was beyond the negativity that we associated them with.

In the times that my mom would speak about this incident, she would always speak hostile about his past actions. "Oh, and I told him to get himself off that street! Before them doggone goblins do! But see, he ain't listen."

But I still couldn't blame him for what he did. The neighborhood that we lived in consisted of continuous violence, numerous thugs, drug addicts, prostitutes, street hustlers, finessers, thots, and mentally ill people. There seemed as if there was nothing but negativity all around. I knew that there were other surrounding areas and blocks that were even worse. Honestly, I felt that if a person from the outside looked at the environment that we currently lived in, they would probably feel that there was no hope, chance to succeed, and even little chance of survival.

That's the way that I felt ever since I was born. I loved Mama to death, but due to the absence of my Father, she was forced to work two jobs just to take care of us. During the day, she worked full-time as a teller and part-time as a cashier for a couple restaurants at night.

Although I knew Mama loved me with all her heart that she had left, she was also absent a good portion of the time that I grew up. Most of the time being home alone Julia and I were responsible for providing for ourselves. I knew Mama would do the best that she could for us whenever she was able to, but we still felt a lack of love which we needed. With this being our situation, I felt like I was put at a big disadvantage already because there was a limited amount of emotional, mental, and financial support in the household.

In our neighborhood, being broke and impoverished was a natural way of life. On top of that, the citizens of our neighborhood felt that it was their duty to get rich off the poor by being robbers, manipulators, and finessers. Julia and I were seldomly allowed to go outside and you could probably guess why. So that neither one of us would end up like our fathers. Julia was my half-sister born to another "dad" that we had at the time, except her father entertained multiple women plus being "committed" to our Mama. This resulted in him pathetically walking out and going ghost on us because he couldn't handle his own sex drive and shame, a few years after when Julia was born.

Julia was almost the exact opposite of me. Most younger people in our neighborhood liked her, she was athletic, and was well respected by her peers even at twelve. She was outgoing, confident, and could attract attention from both genders. "Aye Julia, you so cold at basketball G." They'd say as compared to me. The only attention that I got was negative criticism about everything that was wrong with me. Most of the attention that Julia got was from her basketball skills. Julia played basketball for other outside district programs and was gifted, making her popularity grow at her school and throughout our neighborhood. She also participated in junior track and field events and found success in that too.

With her athleticism, skills, and youth, she was the most bound in our family to be the hope that we needed to get us out of the hood. Out of anyone in our family, whether it was cousins, grandma, aunties, or uncles, it was Julia that had the greatest potential to bring us all out of the hood into a better life. She was the most likely to be the one to get us all the resources that we needed to live a decent life with her goals of becoming a professional athlete.

However, there were a couple of major problems in her aspirations. For starters, like me, Julia's grades were constantly dropping because of the environment we lived in which would make her ineligible from time to time. Other times, she just couldn't make practices or would even miss a few of the games and events because of our day-to-day transportation struggles. After all, we only had one car that Mama would have to use throughout most if not the entire day for work.

Besides the slim chance of Julia becoming a professional athlete, our shortage of income, that Mama would often blame our dads for, was also another obstacle that stood in our way of getting out the hood. Since Mama had to play both roles in the household, her primary focus was on working and paying the bills, which obviously, was a hard task. I remember when Mama would get envelopes from the mail, open them up, and just burst into tears letting her arms drop carelessly on the table pleading, "LORD! PLEASE! You know we ain't got this typa' money!" I remember times where she would quietly consult herself about how she was going to make the next payment without borrowing money or going negative.

One time, I remember her receiving a call from a debt collector. I don't remember the whole conversation, but I remember it going something like this:

Collector: "Ma'am, you owe us and big. So, I would suggest that you find some way. Or we're going to have to…"

Mama: "Look, stop callin' me bout' this bill. I done already told you that I'm gon' pay it back, didn't I?

Collector: "Okay but Ma'am…"

Mama: "OKAY! So, it ain't nomo' discussion about it then. BYE!"

After saying that she hung up the phone and immediately started dialing to call grandma. When grandma picked up the phone after a few rings, I heard Mama practically begging saying, "Come on, Ma. You know we struggling right now." Through the phone, I could hear Grandma respond sternly, "For my grandbabies. And only because of my grandbabies."

Grandma was a strong woman, and I had a great relationship with her, but it was always a gray area between her and Mama. I could never quite understand the relationship between them. They never really spoke about each other to me or Julia. It made things more complicated with grandma living out-of-state, so we rarely saw her. The only times that we did see her were on holidays, special occasions, or the few times we would get to stay with her for a couple days.

Since I never really had an opportunity to see grandma, I would ask mama questions about their relationship growing up. About what grandma had going on in the moment, just to see if I could know more about her since I never saw her all the time like most of the kids, I knew growing up did. I even asked if we could live with her since we were in such a bad environment. But Mama, for whatever reason shot that idea down quickly, saying that God would protect us and keep us safe.

Whenever I would ask about grandma, mama wouldn't offer any real information about her. For   example, I'd ask, "Mama, how's grandma doing?" And she would usually respond, "Oh, she aight." Or I would ask when we would see grandma again. "Aye Ma, when are we going back to grandma's house?" "Oh, don't worry about that baby." She'd respond. On the other hand, when Julia and I would ask Grandma about Mama, she would tell us to just pray for her. "Grandma, what was Mama like as a child?!" We'd ask. "Baby, all I can say is… Just, pray for your Mama okay sweetheart?" Grandma would say in response. Despite the odd connection between Mama and Grandma, I still communicated with grandma on a consistent basis. Multiple times throughout each week she'd usually call me, or I'd call her. Honestly, there were a couple times in my life when I talked to her more than Mama. Not to say that Mama was doing a bad of being a mom, but Grandma set herself in Mama's place as a filler in her absence. She was the main outlet   besides Mama who I could share my thoughts, struggles, and ideas with. She was the one to dust me off when I was dirty, and to calm me through calamity and the insanity that surrounded me throughout my   childhood. It felt as if she was a present mother.

Grandma was also a strong believer in Jesus, Christianity, and the Bible. Literally, every time we would talk, it would result in her telling me to seek God, pray to God, serve God, or use my faith. But more commonly, that God had a unique plan for my life. Far beyond what I could see in my current situation. A plan to be a source for multitudes of people. Out of respect for grandma, I persistently tried all the things that she told me to do when I was younger.

From ages eight to thirteen, I woke up early in the morning and stayed up late to pray to God through Jesus. I've tried, reading my bible, repeatedly, trying to remember and make sense of the scriptures. I went to church listening attentively, trying my best to avoid doing the things that the pastor said was sin. All in an attempt to understand God. Why He would let certain things happen, why He allowed corruption to happen, why He would let me be in the situation that my family and I were in, and to find out what my purpose was. But each time, no result, answer, or clue was given. I couldn't understand the scriptures or make sense of them to save my life. Every time I prayed, I felt as if either God was ignoring me, my prayers weren't making it to Him, or I was just wasting my time. And the more I tried to live "Holy," the more I felt inadequate after realizing that I was still doing something else wrong.

Growing up there was no question in my mind that God was real. It didn't make sense to me how the Earth and its other attributes were formed and created without Him. But that didn't stop me from questioning Him. I knew that I was told to "never question God" but there were a lot of things about God and the way He handled certain situations that, I couldn't understand. One of which was my environment. Why did it seem like the people who did the evilest rarely get punished while the innocent suffered the worst of the impact? But more importantly, why did it seem like bad things always happened to good people and vice versa.

Now don't get me wrong, I still loved Jesus for giving me life and dying for my sins, but I wasn't sure if I was Christian, and I didn't know if God saw me as one of his own children. At least not anymore. Especially after going through all that I've been through and then still dealing with it in my present, I would have thought that by now God would have intervened. But since nothing happened when I prayed, I concluded that He didn't see me as one of His own, even though I tried my best to live my life in a way that was pleasing to Him and would make me a "good" Christian, according to what I was told growing up in church.

I used to pray and ask God to give me some sort of a sign that He was there if He ever was. Asking Him to guide me in the right path and to allow my family and I to be given an opportunity to be put in a better position. But I don't believe

11

that He heard me. It seemed as if every time I prayed for something better things always got worse and this same thing happened to Mama as well.

Once I remember Mama praying for help paying her car note. She had to have prayed for at least three weeks straight with no breaks. Even then, I can still recall the repo man starting to hook up the car to tow it as Mama kept trying to convince him not to. Eventually, she got the man to convince his boss to extend the payment date which she paid off. Which I now know was something that is not supposed to happen, so I attributed God for not allowing our car to be repossessed. It was a miracle to be honest.

I give God credit for allowing us to keep the only car we had to use at the time. But still Mama never found the financial help that she was seeking God for. She ended up having to borrow some small loans, sell some other assets and scrape up the change to pay off the car note. Again, this made me wonder why. Why did God withhold the cash? I thank Him for letting the date get extended, but why did He allow us to feel suffering like this, even when we sought out for Him?

I didn't mean to question God as much as I did growing up because I was always told not to. But there were so many questions that I had. So many things that I did not understand.

All the things I seen Mama go through, and the things that I was going through, I began to feel like God just disliked us as a family. I knew that He is said to love everyone, but I couldn't feel that love, as much as I wanted and tried to, I just couldn't. I was starting to feel like God didn't care, like He had forsaken us. Or maybe, He just wasn't there for us to begin with when I was growing up.

CHAPTER 2: GROWING DOWN

Like in the perfect world shown to us on TV, you'll see the child who is raised by two parents grow up, go to college, get a good job, and start a happy family. Well, I didn't have the luxury of having two parents growing up, and with the frequent absence of my mom, there were times when I felt that I didn't even have one. But more concerningly, I wasn't on the path to go to college or get a good job. Saying that I myself was growing up always seemed like an understatement to me because I never actually felt like I was growing. Of course, I was growing physically and getting older, but it seemed like the older I got, the more responsibilities and needs that came my way that I couldn't handle. I always had more liabilities than assets in my life.

Where I'm from, most young boys had to adapt to becoming a man with little transition. This meant that they would have to find their own way to make money, provide food for themselves, as early as twelve. And the way that they did this was by hustling, selling drugs, stealing, or joining a gang for support. But as you already know, Mama didn't play that with me. So, living the street life to make money was by no means an option for me.

Additionally, there weren't too many people who went to college around me much less finished. Most of those who did go to college went on an athletic scholarship but didn't make it professionally as an athlete and then there were others who went but never finished with their degree, which led them back into trappin'.

The only main professions that the youth in my neighborhood aspired to be were rappers, singers, professional athletes, or some other form of an entertainer like an actor, comedian, dancer, etc. At most, college was seen as an afterthought that could be used for a hook up instead of a tool to find a decent career. What made it even worse was that finishing or even going to college to get a career was of no concern to those in my hood. Most people my age or younger weren't even trying to go and had no plans or desires of getting a professional career and making it out this way. But honestly, it wasn't their fault. There were practically zero real role models from my neighborhood who proved that you could make it out and live wealthy by getting a professional career through education. Where I'm from, the only way to live wealthy was by being an entertainer of some sort or an athlete.

15

Of course, you saw those who did make it out by becoming an entertainer or getting a professional career, but since the relatively small amount of those that did make it out this way were far in between, it made it seem as if this was unachievable.

I wasn't really concerned about what others had going on for themselves. I wasn't worried about what "occupation" those in my neighborhood chose. At times it did concern me, but I knew that the environment of my neighborhood pressured the youth into gaining fast and dishonest wealth. For some, this kind of lifestyle was desired because of the quick and easy way that it could be attained and the potential it had to sustain them in spurts overtime.

I was more concerned about myself. How was I going to make an at least comfortable living for myself and what route was I going to take to get there? First off, I never really did well in school, even when I tried my best, I was still a below average student. So, going the college route was pretty much off the table. Secondly, I wasn't at all athletic and I wasn't skilled in any sports. I wasn't strong, quick, coordinated, or fast and at eighteen being 5'7" weighing a hundred and forty-five pounds, being a professional athlete at a competitive level was out of the question. Thirdly, I had no musical talent whatsoever. I wasn't good at playing instruments and it was a struggle for me any time I ever tried to learn. My singing was awful, my voice would crack when I sang. And I sure enough couldn't rap because I sounded like an old motor trying to start up due to my stuttering. I couldn't dance or keep a beat because I had little rhythm and for a black person that was sad. I was also too shy and passive to be an entertainer and I would get anxiety from standing up in front of big crowds. So, there were no options available for me that I could use to live wealthy. On top of all of this, I already knew that if I ever tried selling drugs or seeking financial support from a gang that Mama would entertain thoughts of kicking me out.

Specifically, I remember once as a child a male stranger in our hood initiated a conversation with me as I walked close to my apartment. After purposefully cutting the conversation short to avoid any conflict that Mama always told me about, I walked back to my crib where Mama met me at the door. "Marlin! Get in the house!" she said sternly. "Boy didn't I tell you not to be talking to them thugs out there?" She said after I had stepped in and closed the door. "But Ma..." "I don't wanna' hear nothing. Now take your behind in that room!" She said interrupting me while I was trying to explain myself. When I got to my room, I heard footsteps following down the hallway with a clinging sound getting louder and with footsteps sounding fiercer, to see Mama appear at my door with a belt. "You gone do right as long as you live in this house." She said. "Now if I ever catch you outside talking to one of them thugs like that again, Imma' beat your lil tail. And if you don't like it, then this house ain't the place for you. I done already told you more than enough times not to be like your father. SO DON'T!" She added before walking away.

I knew it seemed harsh from the outside, but I knew that it wasn't my actions alone that caused this reaction from my Mama. It was the frustration built up from all the men that she allowed into her life, from the "dads" that we had. Of course, I always had to be the target that people took their frustration and anger out on. It was basically the story of my life even as I was coming up in elementary school.

For some reason, when I was coming up in school, my classmates always felt that it was a good idea to target me as the one to take advantage of, to bully, and to pick on. Unfortunately for me, I was an extremely caring, compassionate, and loving kid at heart. This was the total opposite of the people who I knew around me, so it made it hard for me sometimes to fit in. I was one of the ones who was considered "soft." I didn't talk very much and when I did, I would talk at a low tone so that others wouldn't have to hear my stuttering which progressively got worse as I got older.

But don't be fooled, I was no punk. I've gotten suspended at least three or four times and gotten expelled once for fighting. I was a peaceful guy, but for some reason, people always decided to try me by being disrespectful and abrupt. The times that I've fought were out of necessary self-defense. Like I said, people always felt the need to inflict their pain and burdens on to me through verbal and physical abuse. I was the type of guy to avoid conflict and stay to myself for the most part, but I could not stand to be disrespected.

My peers always made fun of me about how I looked, how I dressed, and how I sounded when I stuttered. They'd call me ugly because of my bodily proportions. I had a very scrawny frame yet a large, cube-shaped head. My eyes looked like they were sunken in too far into my face, my teeth, uneven and crooked, and I had a big ole forehead to top it off. And if you're thinking that this was just me being critical on myself, then you should have heard the comments that others made about me at recess. Game-Cube, fivehead, ugly-bugly, was what I was called just to name a few.

Even though it made me mad when they would call me these names, Mama would tell me that no matter how bad I got made fun of, or how much the kids at school taunted me, it was never ok for me to hit them or to fight unless they touched me first. But that would always happen. It would first start out with the name calling. "Oh, Marlin you a this! Marlin you a that! Marlin, you look like a bug!" When I would ignore them, that's when they'd get irritated because they saw that their ways wouldn't prevail and would express it by pushing me or slapping my head. "Boy, you know you heard me." They'd say while touching me and laughing. I never was the aggressive, violent, or impulsive kid who did things that I would later regret when I was in the heat of the moment, but I knew that if I didn't stand up for myself letting these things slide, they would continue and eventually get worse. Usually when these incidents happened, I would end up pushing or slapping them back telling them not to mess with me, which would result in them trying to manhandle me to the ground and escalate into a fight.

In the time that I got expelled, I remember I was attending a local junior high school in my hood. I was in the gym locker room where we had to change from our regular clothes into our gym clothes. When doing so, I remember a kid at the school looking at me up and down and then turning around to his group of friends laughing after every time he looked at me. He repeated this cycle of laughing and staring about four or five times. I ignored it each time, but the more I ignored it the more blatant and disrespectful he became to where others could hear and join in. Being the kind guy that I was, I decided to confront him, "Ay-Ay-Aye man, I-I-I don't wa-wa-want no tra-trouble but..." Before I could even finish my stutter filled sentence, he interrupted me with a forced obnoxious laughter even louder than before. "Aye, y'all hear this boy? Up here stuttering like he scared or sum'." He said to the crowd of people nearby who were listening. "Ma-Ma-Man, w-w-whatever. You, you go...", he slapped me good, point blank as everybody reacted with laughter and yelling, "Ohhh" with amusement.

At that point I couldn't hold my peace any longer, I immediately swung on him with all my force and that's when the fight begun. Since I was always a shorter guy, the guy who picked a fight with me towered me in height and had me by at least twenty pounds in weight. I remember he grabbed me by my collar and shoved me to the ground. On the ground, he got on top of me, and he stood over me holding my shirt yelling in my ear saying how much damage he could do to me if we continued to fight. But I didn't care. I knew I couldn't fight well but I sure enough wasn't going to let him get away with that. So, I rotated around and elbowed him hard which led to us wrestling each other on the ground while everybody cheered and yelled.

That's when the principal walked in and saw me hitting him so that he could get off me. To my surprise, she automatically assumed that I was the aggressor. While the situation was resolved at the principal's office, she noticed his nose was bleeding from when I elbowed him. After asking him what happened and him playing victim, she decided to give him a suspension but decided to give me an expulsion because I was now a "violent person" for hurting him when he was bullying me first, even though I had my share of sores as well.

When I got home, Mama told me that she wasn't at all upset because she knew that I was defending myself. She knew the kind of person I was, the patience that I had with people. She knew she raised me to be respectful to everyone and to be obedient to higher authority. But she also knew that I was likely to be preyed upon in the environment that we were in because of my calm demeanor and innocent appearance.

By no means did I consider myself as a threat or a violent person, but this was rare for a young person in our community. While most kids around me were aggressive, I was passive. While they were violent, I was peaceful. I was polite, they were rude. I was respectful and they were disrespectful.

But I'm not saying this to be bias or to elevate myself above anyone else, I'm being truthfully honest. In my opinion, this isn't even a good thing.

No matter how much I tried to eliminate the excess kindness, compassion, and care that I had for people on the inside, no matter how much I tried to change myself to withstand and compete against the everyday aggression of my neighborhood, it just wasn't enough. I still found myself caring, loving, and respecting people way more than the average person in the hood did. And that bothered me. It bothered me not only because it led me be picked on and taken advantage of but because it made me so different from everyone else. Why? Why was I so different? I know these were all essential emotions and feelings that every human being was supposed to have, but why did I have to have them so strongly and for people that I didn't even know?

What made it even crazier to me was that this wasn't the only way that I was different. There was a decent number of young kids around me who didn't have a specific thought-out plan for their lives. They really didn't know what they wanted to do in life yet. But they were still passionate about things or were talented in things that they themselves could make a living in and have success in. For example, there was a guy who didn't know what he wanted to do for a living or what career he would land in if any. But he was good at playing the piano, he had a gift for it. I asked what he planned on doing for a living when he got older. He said, "Shoot, I don't know. Maybe sum' with music or making beats or sum' like that hopefully." Eventually, he started selling beats to local rappers in our neighborhood for profits and made decent money.

Then there was another guy I knew who had a passion for jewelry and technology. Not necessarily a gift, but a passion. He would find and even steal old jewelry and tech gadgets, refine them and resell them for profits two or three times greater than the original price. Then of course, there were those who claimed that they knew exactly what they wanted out of life. From their perspective, they knew the exact steps they were going to take to get it, and what life they were going to live after they got it. Most of these youngins who had this kind of mindset were those who aspired to be rappers or professional athletes.

However, I was different from all the people mentioned. Different, in a bad way. I didn't know what I was going to do with my life and what I was going to get out of it. I didn't really have a passion for too many things in life like they did. There was nothing that I loved doing so much that I could see myself doing it for the rest of my life. And the things that I did have a passion for like music, sports, and designing, were all things that I knew I wouldn't be able to make any significant amount of money from because I didn't have the intelligence or talent that was needed to do them at a professional level. Whether I did them in the long-term or short-term.

I was also different in a negative sense because I didn't have any real talents or gifts that I could use to sustain myself, no talents to lean upon. While others, even Julia, had gifts, things that they did well with little effort that could allow them to make good money in the future. I didn't have any gifts or special talents that were obvious whenever I was doing them like other people. I was practically ungifted, talentless, and had nothing going for myself. Again, I had this feeling, like God didn't create me for anything special but only to exist. It seemed like He didn't really care that much about me because He basically made me without any gifts. Without a passion for something that I could realistically use to my benefit.

The one thing that I could say that I had a real passion for that could realistically make a way for me was public speaking. I always admired the idea of inspiring others, motivating, and uplifting others through speaking. Offering them support and guidance somewhat like what a pastor, motivational speaker, or life coach does. And no, I didn't want to become a pastor just to scam people out of their money for a living, but these avocations were things that I could see myself doing and enjoying. But as always, there always had to be a major obstacle, a problem for every positive thing with me. And that obstacle was my stuttering. The one thing that I had a real passion for, speaking to inspire others, motivating them by uplifting and encouraging them, and using my words to spread a message, I just had to have this stuttering issue as a hindrance. Any time I would get up in front of people, I was so fearful of stuttering in front of them that I would almost get a panic attack before I even said a word. So, my very last option that I could use to get a comfortable life, gone. My only real passion was stripped away from me by a curse.

So, it brings me back to my initial question. Why was I different in this way? How could others find their niche so easily while I still struggled to find mine? Now that I was going into my senior year of high school, crunch time, the time where everybody starts making plans and deciding what they want to do in life, everybody starts to focus in on perfecting and honing their talents and turning their passions into profits, I was still stuck in sand. I didn't want to force myself into anything that I didn't want or know how to do because I knew

26

that if I were to try and build a life on that, I would hate it. But I was starting to run out of options. None of the possible lifestyles that were available for me to live would keep me financially stable and would still allow me to be safe.

What was I going to do? Was it even possible for me to go to college with the type of grades that I had? How was I going to make it out of the ghetto, if that was even possible for me? How was I going to make a living for myself? I know I couldn't sit around the house or work a minimum wage job that I HATED for the rest of my life. I know I couldn't live the street life, the only lifestyle that seemed available for me, robbing people, selling drugs, or being in a gang. I couldn't live that life, even if I wanted to or even if I was allowed to, I couldn't because I was too caring.

I had no dreams, aspirations, or passions that I could hold on to and hope to see manifest. Not because I was small minded, but because I was convinced that living the "American Dream" and living a successful life wasn't meant for me. I already knew that God didn't choose me for that lifestyle but now, I was questioning the kind of life that He did have for me. By the way things looked, it seemed as if I was leaning towards becoming a plain ole retail or restaurant worker for the rest of my life at best. But at worst, I was starting to become worried that I wouldn't find any way for myself to survive and forsake my upbringing by becoming a criminal or even worse…a bum on the street. I didn't have a direction, clue, or an idea of what I could do to lead my life in a positive direction. Mama always told me to find a decent job, go to school, put my head down and work. But even that was fading more and more into obscurity.

There weren't any good community colleges in my neighborhood, working with my hands to start a trade I knew wasn't a strong suit for me, and we didn't have any consistent way of transportation so that I could get to the decent schools downtown besides public transportation which was always full of some mess, confusion, or drama. Now that I think about it, how would I even have enough money to pay for the cost of tuition? And I didn't want to get any loans because I knew that I wasn't a strong student. It was more than likely that I would end up just going to school, flunking out or barely passing, and then ending up with debt that I couldn't payback and no job because of bad grades which would be a waste!

But worst of all, I felt like I was letting Mama and Grandma down. Of course, they never said it, but in three years from now I couldn't see myself being in a better position. I was starting to feel worried, helpless, hopeless, like a failure. I was fearful of the future rather than excited. I knew that if I never found a way to make myself financially stable, I would be a disappointment. A liability to Grandma and Mama. I didn't understand what my purpose was if I even had one.

This couldn't be me growing up into adulthood. I wasn't growing into anything. I was just going down. Or to be more precise…growing down, and not up.

CHAPTER 3: THE HEAT OF HIGH SCHOOL

High school, the place where incidents happen that fuel adrenaline, and a time were sex hormones run rapid throughout the body. A place where legends are made, where legacies are started, and where they end. A place where teenagers start to express themselves freely and openly by exploring their bodies, their likings, and their emotions. Where memories are made and where events happen that either make or break people for the rest of their lives.

It was the summer before my senior year. Up until this point, my first three years have been terrible to say the least. To begin with, I had low grades as I mentioned before. To be exact, I had a 2.0 GPA and I had gotten an eighteen on my ACT after taking it twice. Now I know what you're thinking:

"Why did you let your grades get that low?"

"Why didn't you get help?"

"You're probably just lazy."

For starters, I wasn't a very intelligent person by nature. I didn't just pick up information and remember it the next day like most of my peers could. Not to say that I was dumb, but I often felt like it compared to my other classmates. What they could learn and remember in a just a matter of minutes took me hours of studying and hard work to understand.

What also didn't help my GPA was the high school that I went to. Oaksenville was out of the neighborhood that I lived in. It was in an upper-class neighborhood that was way better than where I lived. All the wealthy people who were doctors, lawyers, engineers, and educators lived there and sent their children to this school. It was supposed to be some top tier high school where the teachers and school programs were said to be advanced, and the courses were said to prepare their students well for college, offering us "academic support." Well to me, this was all a lie. First off, I always felt that the high school teachers were partial towards me because it always took longer for me to figure things out. I knew that they knew that I didn't exactly live in the neighborhood, and I would often feel like they didn't want me there because of that. They were impatient with me, had bad attitudes when dealing with me, and would get frustrated with me easily telling me that I'll never find a good career if I didn't get any smarter to understand the course material, insinuating to me that I was dumb. Some of them even gave up on me while tutoring telling me that they couldn't tutor me anymore saying," Good luck on the test, Marlin!

31

You'll need it badly." Then walking away while shaking their heads and sighing stressfully.

The curriculum and course work were harder than what I was used to in junior high and elementary back where I lived, so it was a rough adjustment that I couldn't grasp yet. The class workload was also way more than what I received back in junior high. Additionally, with many of the students coming from wealthy households, it made them flashy and snobbish. Now I'll admit, the school was racially diverse, having blacks, whites, Asians, etc. But the blacks at my school were spoiled rotten but pretended to be street kids while flashing their clothes and jewelry in each other's faces, a behavior they learned from famous rappers. The whites often had their own cliques as well but still merged with the other black students. Although they weren't as flashy, they were still snobbish in a sense and were hyper focused on their grades.

Then there was me. The outcast. I couldn't fit in with the black cliques because I was the opposite of flashy, never having the money to buy anything significant for myself which resulted in me getting ridiculed by them, my own people. And of course, I couldn't fit in with the whites because I wasn't "white" enough for them. I had nothing that I could relate to with them. This, I knew, also affected my grades because I was always being rejected and talked about during school hours because I was, as you would guess, different. This would distract me from focusing on learning, which was already hard enough.

So technically speaking, I wasn't black enough to hang with the black kids and I was too black to roll with the white kids. I know, crazy right. Well, it was Mama's idea. Mama wanted me to get a good education so that I could get into a good college. And she was kind of mad that it wasn't working out so well. But thanks to Grandma, I was still able to go and give it one last chance by entering my senior year to try and pull my GPA up as much as I possibly could. It was Grandma who helped Mama pay for me to go to the school that I went to, but we still had to pretend that I lived at one of Mama's friend's houses by using her address to make it seem like I lived in that neighborhood.

On top of that, I worked two part-time jobs up until this point. I worked my job before I even entered my freshmen year of high school so that we wouldn't have to go without hot water, heat, and things of that nature. However, working part-time would cause me to have a shortened time for things like studying, doing homework, and attending tutoring sessions, putting me at an even worse disadvantage. It already took me long enough to try and understand the course material on my own, and now that my time, which should have been used to study or receive tutoring, was being cut even shorter, it left me with a small-time frame to try and make sense of schoolwork that was already challenging. All the while, the other kids at my school could focus solely on their schoolwork having everything that they needed and got the things they wanted when they wanted it.

Although you had to be at least sixteen to get a job where I was from, I was able to get my first job shortly after turning fourteen sweeping and cleaning at the local barber shop on some weekdays and weekends. I hated seeing the way that Mama struggled earlier in my childhood trying to provide for us by working overtime and over working herself, which is what motivated me to get a job before I was even "old enough." The barber shop that I used to work at was right down the street, maybe about a quarter mile from my house, so it gave me the benefit of avoiding the spots that were conducive for gang activity. Since I didn't have to go that far to get to work, Mama didn't mind me working there to help her with the bills.

Dale, the owner of the shop was an older man in his late seventies. He was the one who hired me after I told him about my situation. He took to me and took me under his wing, almost as if I was his own son. Unfortunately, his only biological son had died at the tender age of eighteen to gang violence. So, when he looked at me, he often told me that I reminded him of his son. Not having a father in my life, that meant a lot to me, and was one of the few positives in my life. He always told me about having hope and perseverance. Hoping for a better day to come, even though I couldn't see it currently. Which was strange because that was like what Grandma would always tell me. "There's value beyond your visual, young blood, remember that." He'd always say to me when I talked to him.

I'd work for him at his shop and receive a monthly stipend of a hundred and fifty dollars all of which I would give to my Mama so she could make ends meet and continue to provide the basic needs of the household. It went well while I worked for Dale at his shop until I turned sixteen. One day while at work a man came into the shop and recognized one of the clients that was in the chair getting his hair cut. As soon as the client being serviced saw the man who walked in, he immediately jumped out of his chair to attack him, with his cape still on. That's when they began to fight. It took all the barbers who were working that day to break up the fight and calm them down. After the situation was resolved and the police showed up, it was revealed that the two previously had beef, over some woman that they both had in the past. Thank God that neither one of them had a gun that day as people getting killed by gun violence was the norm.

After this situation occurred, Dale decided to move his shop over to a better part of Chicago in a safer area, which forced me to quit and find a new job. This also made Mama worry because she was so afraid of me getting hurt if I was to try and work at another local barber shop or store. So, I looked and looked, trying to find a job that wasn't doing something terrible like having to work outside in bad weather conditions or things like that. After about a month of searching, I found a job in the neighborhood where I was attending High-School thanks to the recommendation from Thomas, one of the few friends that I had in school.

This job is where I now currently work. It's a restaurant that focuses on pleasing the customer by any means, even at the expense of every employee's mental and physical health, dignity, character, morals, and values. The customers come first before any of the employees no matter what and most employees are looked at as slaves. It's been nearly two years, but I was already sick of this job since my second week. I remember Thomas telling me about how easy it was to get a job there because no one stayed long term, and people got fired all the time, that's how bad it was. To put it in perspective, I served in two different roles within my job, being a table cleaner, and occasionally being a door greeter when we would get busy. I got paid minimum wage but worked at a rapid pace alternating between the two jobs doing both in one shift some of the time. The managers were horrible and showed no respect towards me and the employees, who were antisocial. The employees were only concerned about themselves, and rude to each other because they were all depressed about being there.

In addition, I was one of a few black people who worked there, the others worked morning shifts while I only worked during evenings and nights. And with most of the customers being white as well, I always felt a sense of racism towards me from every angle. The bottom line was that the job was terrible. It didn't include that many benefits unless you were a chef or manager, and although most of the customers were wealthy, they were still cheap, so I rarely got any tips. I remember once it was an extremely busy day where people were coming in all at once. I was busy clearing table after table while the manager, Mike, who seemed as if he hated me even though he had absolutely no reason to, observed me working hard. As soon as I put my head up, there he was standing in front of me staring like he was some type of ninja warrior.

"Don't just sit there lookin' at me, HURRY UP! Then when you're finished, go hold that door for the incoming customers." He said to me while customers turned their heads to see what was happening.

First off, I was a hard-working employee and I even remember sweating that day from moving around so much. Then he tells me about making myself useful, please, if it wasn't for me then there would be no one to make use of. But, as Mama raised me to be respectful to those above me and to be humble, I tolerated this mess all the time and continued doing my job. I went to the door and started holding it for people. According to the restaurant policy, it was the greeter's job to not only open the door but greet the incoming customers as well by welcoming them to the restaurant stating the name of it and saying how well the service was. Well, as you may already know, I stuttered badly so I decided to greet the incoming customers with just saying hello. When the manager saw this, he stormed over to me to make sure that I was following the restaurant policy by getting close in my ear and saying, "Greet. Them. PROPERLY!" He started off speaking at a low tone but getting louder with each word.

Again, trying to do my best as an employee out of how I was bought up, I obeyed. Upon opening the door for the next group of customers who walked in, I tried to greet the customers "properly" starting by welcoming them. As they came in, I proceeded to say, "welcome" but as I began to say it, I started stuttering, "Weh-Weh-Weh-Weh-We-Welcome…" And as soon as the incoming customers heard this, they laughed right there in my face like I wasn't even there. I felt so disrespected, and this wasn't the only time something like this happened to me.

There were so many times where I wanted to quit my job and walk off. Times where I wish I could fight the unfair managers. But I knew that if I did either one of these, that I would permanently lose this job and my family and I would have to go back to struggling even worse than now. That's why this whole time, I was trying to find a new job. Not necessarily a better job, because I felt that any job besides this one would be better. But for some reason, even something seemingly that simple was so hard for me. I applied for other similar low-end jobs that paid more money but were basically the exact same thing that I was doing now.

No response. Retail or warehouse jobs, no reply. And the jobs that did reply and interviewed me, I would get so anxious and stutter so bad throughout the entire interview that the interviewers decided to cut the interview short. Which I knew was the cause of me not getting the job due to my inability to communicate effectively.

I felt stuck, like I was trapped. Why was I so unfortunate? It was like no matter how hard or how much I worked, we were still broke. No matter how hard I tried in school, my grades were still low. I've been working at this crazy job for two years now working about twelve to fifteen hours a week making less than six-hundred dollars a month, still giving the bulk of it to Mama and still seeing her struggle. I was still lacking the things that others had that they didn't even have to work or pay for. It was frustrating. It took even longer for me to get from home to work now that I've worked at this restaurant, since it was out of the neighborhood.

My first three years of high school has been negative until now and it didn't look like it was going to get any better. My GPA was at a rock bottom due to me being cursed with intelligence that was far below average and being put in a school with "teachers" who didn't really care to help or care if I failed. I was constantly being ridiculed by my own people for not being like them and being rejected by the other groups of people because I was misunderstood by them. I was targeted for slander because I was "ugly", which shifted my focus from prioritizing school to focusing on avoiding conflict. I practically had no choice but to work myself to the bone while being underpaid so that my family and I won't have to barely survive but have a chance at living and so that Mama won't have to borrow from others or overwork herself.

I wasn't trying to make excuses for myself, but again, experiencing all of this felt like punishment and made me go back to the question that I've been asking all my life. Why me? Why did God choose me to have all these disadvantages? Why wasn't He there for me? Why did He choose me to have all these flaws?

Below average intelligence. Being hated because I was different and talked about because I was the below the standards of others. Isolated and disliked for no reason. Even when I treated others with respect, I still wasn't treated fairly. I didn't understand the reason behind what I was going through because to my understanding, I remained humble, always. I minded my own business and didn't bother anybody. I was respectful and I've learned how to refrain from my emotions that would cause me to get into fights during heated moments. I genuinely had love and cared for other people even those that I didn't know, which I know was kind of weird to others around me, but that's just who I was. I did my best to provide for my family for the past three years to make up for the absence of my father. Although I didn't pray as much as I know that I should have, I still had a genuine love for Jesus. But in going through what I was going through, my question was, did He still have that same love for me? I knew that God loved everybody. I know that He had love for his creation, but I felt like I was the last of His concerns. I was feeling like He made me with little to no regard or care.

I was coming up on my first day of senior year. I had one week left until class started. I had just come home from a full day of work, and it was later in the evening when I got a phone call from grandma.

Me: "Hey Grandma. Wha-Wha-What's go-going on? H-h-h-how ya been?"

Grandma: "Hey baby, I been good, God is good! How about you?"

Me: "Ya-Ya-Yea, I-I've b-ba-been ok."

Grandma: "That's good. What you over there doing?"

Me: "Oh, uh, I-I-I juh-juh-just ga-ga-got ha-ha-ha-home from work."

Grandma: "Oh ok, my hard-working grandson. I heard you was about to start school pretty soon."

Me: "Yea, I-I-I-I-I'm trying t-t-to g-g-get ready fa-fa-for it. Bu-but I know it's p-p-probably gone b-b-b-be a-a-a-another long ya-ya-year."

Grandma: "Well that's ok baby as long as you do your work, stay focused, and ask questions, you can continue your education in college. Have you thought about what you might do after High-School?"

Me: (After a moment of silence) "Weh-Well, to be honest...I still don't really nut-nut- know yet. But I-I-I-I've b-b-been th-th-thinking a-a-about it."

Grandma: "Well don't wait on it too long now, sweetheart. You don't want to end up not having a place to go if you gonna' go to college."

Me: "Gra-Gra-Grandma, ca-ca-can I be honest? Like real real honest?"

Grandma: "Of course, sweetheart. Go ahead."

Me: "Like... (sigh and brief pause) I don-don't...I-I-I-I just don't know wa-wa-what I wa-wa-wanna do Ma. Like, I-I-I tried praying, I tried reading tha-the bible, but I still don't know. I tried everything you-you-you said Ma."

Grandma: "That's good son. But you gotta believe it for yourself too now baby. You have to see yourself overcoming, see yourself rising above your visuals. See past what you see now. Because there's value beyond your visual. Every obstacle and challenge that you face, every setback that comes to you in life, that's a visual and there's something valuable that God has waiting for you on the other side of it. Walk by faith Marlin, and not by sight."

Me: "Yea I ga-ga-guess... I guess I just b-b-b-been d-d-down on myself lately."

Grandma: "That's ok, it's not about where you are in life right now, it's about where you choose to stay. And if you decide to stay in that place, how you expect God to get you out if you are content and comfortable with where you are. Keep seeking Him. Don't give up. And you'll see Him move. You never have to accept the low places in life just push past them."

Me: "Yea, tha-tha-that's a good p-p-point."

Grandma: "Alright now baby, I know you tired so imma let you get your rest. Ok?"

Me: "Ok."

Grandma: "Alright bye bye sweetheart. I love you and I'm always praying for you."

Me: "Alright, th-th-thanks Grandma, for everything. An-an-an-and I luh-luh-love you too. Ta-talk to you later."

Grandma: "Alright bye-bye."

After getting off the phone I went and got in the shower to wash off the sweat and musk. I started to think about the things Grandma told me over the phone. It's not about where I am but where I stay. Yea that sounded all fine and dandy, but it wasn't like I was trying to stay in my position anyway. It's not that I wanted to stay in the position that I was in or that I was content in it, of course I didn't want to be in my current situation. But what were the options that I had that would allow me to leave? What positives did I have that I could use to my advantage? In the past, every time I tried to believe God, even for something that seemed as if it was small, it seemed like it never went in my favor. It felt like God was far off. I had no options, and I was now being convinced that maybe I was meant to be in this situation, maybe I wasn't meant to get out and live a comfortable life. But what did I ever do to deserve this?

Besides the fact, on a very dim bright side, I knew I still had one last shot going into my senior year. Although this shot didn't have a clear target view, it was still a shot. So, I figured I'd just take the bullet, load it up, shoot for the stars that I couldn't see and see what happens. Realistically, I practically had a zero percent chance of getting all A's or even getting all A's and B's this year, but like Grandma said, it's not about where I am or where I start, it's about where I stay. And if I stayed at this 2.0 GPA, I'd stay in this position which would stop me from going to a college disallowing me to have a career and getting out of the hood. As much as I thought that I couldn't make it out, there was still that feeling, that one percent feeling of optimism that I had within me, which made me feel that I could make it out. And to make it out through having something professional, which would be an uncommon yet fulfilling feat.

When I got out of the shower to dry, I looked at myself in the mirror and thought, "I will make it out. I will bring up my grades and go to college or at least find something." No matter what obstacles that tried to come, despite the distractions or hindrances, I thought of myself overcoming them and envisioned myself doing it. At this moment, I set my mind on getting into college by facing the heat that my senior year had for me. The heat of high school could burn me alive, but I decided that this day, I will be a conqueror and a survivor. Whatever it took for me I was willing to do it because this was my only option, and I knew that I had to work for it. I understood that it wouldn't be easy, and that it was sort of late. But it was better now than never. I knew that even if I were to get exceptional grades that it still wouldn't be enough to get me into a quality college. Matter of fact, I knew that it would probably get me into a low-end college if I even got good grades this year. But it would be a start which was all that I needed, a start. I could figure out the rest later, but if I could at least get accepted into a college, I could for once have a weight lifted off my shoulders.

So, I put on a mental firefighter suit so that my mind could withstand the heat of high school. Because I had to find a way out, a way to escape, and this was the only option that I knew of. I decided to put my trust in God to help me with school and help me get my grades up. I thought to myself, "God, I know I don't trust you as much as I should, but if you allow me to make it out of the hood safely through education, I owe you everything."

I didn't know exactly how I was going to do in school this year, but I decided to trust and believe God, something that I haven't done in a little while, to give me the smarts and the grace to overcome. I needed to overcome all the obstacles that stood in the way of me achieving my new goal of graduating high school and going to college to make it out of the hood. Although I despised school, I knew that it could benefit me if I would incorporate faith into my studies which would ease the difficulty of school and academics. I had to get out. I had to find a way to not just survive or exist, but to live. One way or the other.

CHAPTER 4: STARTING ON A FINISHED PROJECT

My alarm woke me at 5:55am. It was the first day of my senior year. Since I went to school outside of the neighborhood, I had to take two buses to get to school in addition to walking to get to the bus stops. My class started at 7:30am, so I had an hour and thirty-five minutes to get there on time. Mama had to be at work at eight and couldn't drop me off at school since she as well had to travel outside of our neighborhood. For her to be on time, she would leave around 7:15am. So, by the time that she would leave, I'd already be on my way to school.

I peeked into Julia's room to see if she was awake just to see her knocked out sleeping with her arms spread out across the bed. I went to the bathroom to brush my teeth. After I finished, I went into the kitchen to see if there was a breakfast snack around, to see Mama sitting at the kitchen table drinking her coffee. "Hey baby." She said. "Hey Ma." I responded. "It's your first day of school, I just can't believe it. You're a whole senior now!" She said. "Ye-Ye-Yea, I-I-I know. It's crazy." I responded.

She asked if I was ready for my final year. I responded that I had no choice but to be ready and to get ready because this was my last chance to find a direction for life before I enter full blown adulthood. After pausing and then positioning herself so I could hear her clearly, she finally said, "Remember what I told you? Always be humble. Stay away from this 'street life' son. Stay away from this so called hustlin', these gangs, these drugs. It's not worth it, trust me, I know. You're capable of more than that." She said. "This is the same thing that I told your father, but you see where it took him. That's why I'm telling you, I don't wanna see you, another man in my life, shoot, any man out here, fall into the pits of the street. Work hard, focus, stay in school, and it will take you far." She added.

After hearing her say that it made me think about the life that Mama lived before, she had me. The unknown past that she had. Mama never really talked about her childhood or how she was bought up and neither did my grandma. I knew a few things about it but like I said, the relationship between them was a blur and so was the past of my Mama. Literally, anytime I'd ask her about her childhood and how she grew up it would result in her giving me basic responses with little to no detail. Other times she would just question me about why I needed to know. But out of respect for Mama, I never tried to figure it out or tried to trick her into telling me by constantly asking, I just kept myself guessing and wondering.

But it dawned on me, I had to be the only child who grew up knowing nothing about the childhood of their parents. Other kids who I grew up with would always talk about the things that their parents used to do when they were growing up. It seemed as if they knew their parents so well that they had written a whole bibliography of them and were present when they were growing up. For me, however, that was never the case, so I let my mind roam in its curiosity of Mama's upbringing.

I continued to get ready by taking a quick shower and looking through my closet trying to find an outfit to wear in my limited wardrobe. I threw on some khakis and a flannel shirt as always. Since Mama couldn't give me a ride to school, I would start my journey by walking to the first bus stop to take the city's public transportation. Ideally, I would have liked to take an uber but since I had to do this routine every day to get from school and back, paying for such services each time wouldn't be a smart financial decision. So, taking the bus in combination with walking was the cheapest way for me to get to school.

Typically, I would leave the house and take a ten to fifteen-minute walk to get to the bus. Since it was so early in the morning, there wasn't a lot of threats as far as criminals and gangs, but I still avoided the areas where I knew would be a hotspot for mischief. I would arrive at the bus stop about five minutes early and get on the bus riding it until I got closer out of the hood into the nicer neighborhoods, which took approximately ten minutes. Then, I would have to take another ten-minute walk to get to the school bus stop. After stopping at everyone's stop, I would end up at school with enough leisure time before class started.

This year on this day, my very first day, was no different. After doing all of this, I finally arrived at school for my first day of my senior year. I was anxious, nervous, and hyped all at the same time. Butterflies were flying all around in my belly, and it felt as if my heart was pounding outside my chest. Usually, I would spend that leisure time in the library to try and rush to catch up on all the homework that I didn't complete and to also avoid being seen. But since it was the first day, I didn't have to worry about any of that, so I decided to just browse the school to see what was new. After all, it was two and a half months since I had last been there.

So, I proceeded to walk around. While doing so, it seemed as if every other person that I passed was with another person, of the opposite sex, hugging, rubbing, and kissing them. Now this was a slight exaggeration, but it seemed like everybody was "boo'd up" or was in a relationship. Now, I wasn't jealous of them, but seeing that just made me want that kind of relationship since I never had a real girlfriend in my entire life. And it wasn't just because I wanted sex. It wasn't because I wanted to be seen with somebody else, I just wanted something, someone. Someone to love and someone to love me.

See, growing up being considered ugly really took a toll on me mentally, and on my confidence. *"Oh, but Marlin, you supposed to be a young cat from the hood. You don't need no love or even supposed to have them feelings,"* is probably what some people from my hood would say or think if I ever shared these thoughts or feelings with them. But everyone in this world needs love. Everyone in this world wants to feel appreciated by a significant other. Everyone in this world needs validation and affirmation in some way and I was no exception.

As I walked over to my locker to get situated for class, I heard some chuckling from behind me. I ignored it at first because I figured that it was probably just another couple enjoying their lust for each other. But as I kept hearing it, I also heard one of them say while giggling, "Look at his hair. (Laughing) Oh, look at this man's shirt, that boy extra wrinkled. (More laughing)" And that's when I came to the conclusion that were talking about me. So, I turned around slightly and looked over my shoulder, and sure enough they were looking at me and pointing.

Since this happened often, this one little incident didn't bother me as much because I was already used to it. I was just trying to stay focused on the goal that I entered with. The goal of going all out in my studies and my grades through the grace of God to get into a college and out of the hood. As long as I kept that goal and pursued it, I knew that other small incidents like this wouldn't be a major concern to me.

The time came for me to get to my first class. I always liked to be early and be the first person in the class so that I could see everyone who walked in. I walked into my first class which was English. I was the second person who walked into the class, so I put my bag down and sat in the back of the class. The teacher nodded his head as I sat down to show that he acknowledged me and continued typing on his computer. I watched as people started to stroll into the classroom and get situated. Before I knew it, three fourths of the classroom was full. And that's when the bell for class rung.

The teacher got up and started to greet the class and began pulling out the attendance sheet to take roll call. As he started to do that, I saw someone walk through the door who I never expected to see. Ashley, an old childhood friend. Ashley and I grew up together when she lived in the hood with me. From about ages ten to thirteen, she went to the same school as me and that's how we got close. She was one of the few people back then who actually wanted to be my friend and spend time with me. Sometimes, Mama would even let me go over to her house so her mom could take us downtown to hang out.

Eventually, a little after Ashley turned thirteen, she started to act a bit strange towards me. Sometimes she would get an attitude with me for no reason and other times she would seem irritated when I was talking to her. Halfway through eighth-grade year, Ashley moved out of the hood because her mom found a new job in the suburbs that paid well, and her parents got back together.

I recognized her by her unique features. Ashley was a caramel-skinned black girl with hazel eyes and frizzy hair. She looked EXTREMELY different from the last time that I saw her almost five years ago. When Ashley and I were growing up, she was considered to be one of the "ugly" girls in junior high even though I still found her attractive. She wore glasses, had braces, was very thin, and had nappy hair. Sort of like me which is why I think we got along so well in the beginning. But now Ashley looked totally different. She had lost her glasses and her braces having an almost perfect facial structure and nice teeth. Her face and skin were clear as a pure waterfall. Her natural hair was now long, straight, and was almost a completely different texture. Her body had filled out to being built like that of a female superhero in a comic book or movie. Her style and taste had changed from before, wearing fancy, expensive designer clothes that she never had when we grew up. Bottom line, the girl was FINE!

Now that pretty much everyone was in class, the teacher began calling out names for roll call. After calling the first few names, he shouts, "Marlin Lewell?" As I raised my hand, I see Ashley turn her head in my direction, look at me, and stare, looking as if she recognized me. I gently smiled at her and threw my hand up to wave at her. After seeing this, she just glanced at me up and down and looked away without showing any sign of greeting or acknowledgement.

"What's wrong with her." I thought to myself. Does she think that she's too good for me or something? I didn't want to jump to conclusions but that's the only reason why I think that she would respond to me in this way. But anyways, as the teacher continues roll call and finally gets to Ashley, he shouts, "Ashley Wittmanton?", and when she said "here" all the guys who saw her in the classroom started looking at each other smiling liked they were shocked by what they saw. That's when my mind started to think so many things about the future that me and Ashley could possibly have. What if I talked to her? I mean, we were already friends before. So, what would be the problem if I spoke to an old friend? I knew all the guys liked her, but I had an advantage over all of them because we knew each other already. Besides, I was a young man, so it's natural for a young man to have female friends, right?

As I was thinking, I saw another student walk into class, and I immediately knew who he was. Deon Riceton Jr., son of a retired basketball player. Deon had to be the most popular dude at school. Ever since he was a freshman he's been well known for his athletic abilities. Deon was a starter on our varsity basketball team since his freshman year and was the star wide receiver for our football team since sophomore year. He had to be about 6'4" weighing around 200lbs. The dude was like a solid rock in his physique with veins and cuts all in his arms. He was also mixed with his Father being black and Mother being white. He was light skinned but with bluish eyes and long brown fluffy hair that was in a man bun.

When he walked in the teacher greeted him by saying, "Deon, I'm ecstatic that you're in my class." Deon, smiling, just walked to an open seat. The teacher then opened class by welcoming us back to school. As an icebreaker, he asked basic questions about our personal lives. In one of the questions, he asked if it was anyone's first year at Oaksenville and Ashley raised her hand. The teacher prompted her to share about the school she attended previously and where she was from. After saying the name of her previous school, Ashley confidently proceeded to say, "And I'm from the projects."

The class, looking surprised, quietly chattered amongst themselves while snickering before Ashley responded saying, "What? Y'all ain't never seen a girl from the hood before?!" "Nah, we just ain't seen one this fine!" Shouted Deon across the classroom as the whole class, even the teacher, reacted with laughter. After saying this, I saw Ashley start to make a face at Deon as if she was flattered by what he said, smirking at him while looking at him thoroughly up and down.

"Deon, since you made quite the scene here, why don't you tell the class a little bit about yourself, since you have already said what's on your mind." The teacher said. Deon, responding, says sarcastically, "Well, in case y'all ain't know, my name is Deon. I get bad grades in school, I'm terrible at sports, and I like sitting at home on the couch eating pizza all day." The teacher laughs and says, "Class I know most of you guys already know, but he's the opposite of everything he said."

Yea, the teacher was right, Deon was blessed to be born smart and athletic. He was always on the honor roll, even when he was still in season. A news article that I read about him stated that he had a 3.7 GPA while taking courses like engineering and advanced calculus in addition to dominating in athletics, being known throughout the state for his skills on the court and the field. He was also said to have over three hundred thousand dollars in scholarship offers, for athletics in basketball and football combined, from highly ranked schools in the country. And if that wasn't enough, there were debates amongst high school sports newscasters about where he would go after high school and where he could possibly be drafted after college to the NBA.

But within the school, Deon was known and praised for his character. Despite him being famous on social media and popular in school, Deon was a very friendly person, although I never encountered or interacted with him in school, I saw how he treated everyone that he interacted with. With respect and value. He was sociable with the "lame kids", with special needs kids, the nerds, and the middle-class kids. Whether you were quiet, outgoing, popular, or not, wealthy, or not, Deon was going to be respectful to you. And I've seen it for myself, he would go around greeting people and complimenting them just to be friendly.

Unlike the other popular athletes at school, who tried to be bullies, Deon was different. This is why I respected him the most although I didn't know him personally. For this very reason, all my peers at school loved him because he used his outgoing personality and popularity to reach others. It was deeper than sports with him; it was about connecting with others too.

As the teacher continued with class, he eventually informed us of an assignment that was going to be due in a few weeks. This assignment was worth a large portion of our semester grade. It was a speech assignment where we had to pick a poetic story, memorize it, and perform it in front of the class for points that were worth a large chunk of our overall grade. The teacher told us that if we did poorly on this, then it could be hard for some to recover. For this reason, he encouraged us to get a head start on it. Great. I already struggled to remember things and you already know how I sound when I talk. But mentally, I told myself that I would stay committed to my goal, and I wasn't going to let any of these small hinderances keep me from accomplishing it. So, I decided that I would start as soon as I got home, because I was determined to use every opportunity that I had to bring my GPA up.

Before I knew it, class was over after the teacher handed us the syllabus and reminded us to work on our speech assignment. The bell rung and everybody started clearing their desks and grabbing their bags to leave for their next class. Since we had about ten minutes in between classes and my next class was right around the corner, I decided to take my time getting there. I glanced over at Ashley and observed how all the guys in the class looked at her with lust while they were walking out of class. After half of the class left, I saw Deon make his way over to her and introduce himself. With a smile, she offered him a handshake as the two continued to walk out the classroom together talking side by side.

After I walked out, I realized that my locker was close to Ashley's locker where she was talking to Deon. I stood back and watched from a short distance how they talked and flirted while some of Deon's athlete friends began to crowd him. One of them being Jack, another senior who played for our high school basketball team. As Jack and Deon did their little handshake, I saw Jack eyeballing Ashley. Jack was a tall white guy, who was about 6'6", and although he wasn't as built as Deon, he was still considered attractive by most of the girls in the school. He was what you would call the "bad boy" type and although he was white, he was very comfortable being around blacks and seemed as if he had a black soul. As I watched, I saw Deon introduce Jack to Ashley as they locked eyes and shook hands. And by the way that they locked eyes, it was obvious that they as well had chemistry.

Another one of Deon's friends who crowded him was Freida. Freida was actually Deon's girlfriend, supposedly, but there were multiple rumors about how Deon would cheat on her with other girls in the school. Although these were just rumors with no supporting evidence, it was obvious to me that it was true because of how Deon interacted with Ashley. Nevertheless, Freida remained loyal to Deon through it all. Now Freida was a beautiful chocolate dark skinned girl. She had a thick, curvy body which made her a desirable target for most guys in the school. Although she was considered to be one of the nicer people who went to our school, she always closed the door to any possibilities of a side relationship that could emerge through flirting from other guys. She was a cheerleader on the cheerleading team and cheered well. She had a bubbly energetic personality and was said to be a "white girl in a black girl's body."

I sat back and watched as Deon's group of friends socialized while various people shouted Deon's name from afar during the passing period. Suddenly, I saw Ashley's head turn in my direction. She looked back at me and then to her new group of friends then back at me again. She did this a couple times, making faces hinting that I was making her uncomfortable by looking at her. Likewise, the rest of the people in the group who she was socializing with did the same. After her third turn, that was when I perceived that she may have realized that I was watching her from afar which was the cue for me that I should go on my way. As I did so, after passing by their group trying not to be noticed to avoid conflict, I heard Jack yell, "Aye, Aye bro...! What's his name? (Asking one of the people in his group.) Aye, Marlin! Come here!"

I looked over my shoulder as I saw everyone from their group staring at me intently while Jack motioned his hand signaling that he wanted me to come over. Something in my mind told me not to go over there, but my non-thinking self decided to do it anyway. As soon as I got there, Jack immediately said, "Aye, look man, I know you're probably looking over here because you want to be over here with us, which is cool, but don't be staring at us like you on to something, alright?" "Awe na-na-nah boy, I-I-I a-ain't on nut-nut-nothing, I na-na-know her." I said while pointing to Ashley.

After I said this, Deon, and Jack both looked at Ashley for a response. "Yea, I used to know him." Ashley said, sighing while getting an attitude. Despite having a minimal confidence in myself, I nervously stretched out my hand to Ashley thinking and hoping that she would shake it and remember how we used to hang out with each other growing up. All while stuttering saying "Heh-ha-heh-heh-hey, A-A-A…" and before I could even get her name out of my mouth, Deon shoved me with one hand saying, "Boy, she don't wanna' talk to yo' ugly lil' self." Although Deon used little effort to push me, he was so strong that I ended up losing my balance, tripping over my own foot nearly falling on the ground in front of everyone in the hallway.

Everyone who crowded Deon chuckled, including Ashley. "Deon?!" I heard Freida say with concern. My initial thought was to get up and start unleashing on Deon but there were two things that immediately popped up in my mind after being pushed down that stopped me. One, if I got up to fight Deon, I knew I would automatically lose because he was nearly twice the size of me and two, if I did fight, I knew I would get suspended which would cause me to forfeit my last chance to accomplish my only available goal of going to college by retaliating to foolishness. So, I decided to be the bigger person by letting it slide and tolerating it.

"Dang bro, you didn't have to push him down like that." Jack said while I got myself together and stood up. "I didn't push him, I just tapped him. (Talking to me.) My fault bro. What's your name? Marlin?" Deon asked me with false sincerity, pretending to feel guilty seeing that he had knocked me down. "Ye-ye-yea, Marlin." I replied. "You know I was just playing around, right?" He asked with a smirk as he reached out to shake my hand. "S-s-s-shut up b-b-b-b-boy." I said in irritation, staring at him angrily while smacking his hand away from me. In doing so, I saw Ashley continue to just stand there with her arms folded scrolling through her phone, like she didn't even care about what happened and that we used to be friends. After seeing how I responded, Deon then wiped the smirk off his face and stared back at me with a serious face before turning back around to his group. I gathered myself and walked to my next class watching everyone look at me as they passed by because of what had just happened.

As mad as I was, I was also confused. Deon was supposed to be one of the nicer people in our school who had good character and treated everyone fairly. I've seen it for myself, there were times where he would literally go around and greet people who weren't popular just for the sake of being friendly. It was disappointing because I respected him for how he treated others but now, he mistreated me. If I didn't have this new aspiration of going to college, I would have fought him, whether I would have lost or not. I would have fought him not because I wanted to get attention, but because that was flat out disrespectful. I didn't even say anything to him, and he pushed me to the ground.

But now coming to think about it, it was strange to me that he was respectful to everyone else but me. Then it hit me, maybe he wasn't really a super nice or respectful guy like he portrayed. Maybe he was painting a false image of himself just to boost his overall status being the athlete that he was. Now it was starting to make sense, he wasn't really a super loyal, respectful, and flawless person like he portrayed himself to be. If he was, he wouldn't have tried to push me down like he did. But since he was well respected by everyone, because he was athletic and "nice" to everyone, what difference would it make to him if he treated one person poorly. And of course, that one person was me, a nobody. So, what he did to me wouldn't have any effect on him. But why me? It must've been something about me that made him dislike me and it wasn't just because I was a lame. So, I thought on this until the next class got started.

After getting through all my morning classes, it was finally time for lunch. We had multiple options to choose from for lunch in the cafeteria, with each meal averaging around at least six or seven dollars. In the past, there were days that I would be able to afford a whole meal but there were other days where I could only afford a bag of chips and a soda to be the most financially beneficial to myself. Either way, I was thankful to be able to eat as there were times in my childhood where Julia and I went to bed hungry. This year, I knew, would be no different. So instead of buying myself a meal, I went and got into the snack line. Across the cafeteria, I saw my friend Thomas standing in the line to get a meal. I was staring directly at him as he was standing in line looking around the cafeteria. When we eventually saw each other, he casually waved as I nodded my head upwards.

Thomas pointed out an empty table for us to sit at. Thomas was probably one of my only real friends at school. He was extremely relatable even though he came from a rich background. He saw things the same way that I did and didn't want to be a part of cliques. I didn't have a lot of friends, and neither did Thomas, but there were two friends of his who weren't really friends of mine. Thomas told them during lunch to come sit with us. They came and sat with us when they located us.

I didn't consider friends Dawson or Casper friends but rather acquaintances. Since we all knew each other already, we greeted each other by doing our handshakes. Dawson and Casper considered themselves to be my friends, but I knew that they weren't really in my corner. Casper was half Filipino and half Irish and was known for his ability to roast others, but he was sneaky about it. There were times when I would be talking, and he would say something to throw shade at me and discredit what I was saying. Dawson was the kind of a "so called friend" as I put it, to me. He always "joked" about the flaws and imperfections of a person, but he was bolder about it. He made sure to do that with me. Although I never really got offended by it, there were times I had to check him about his behavior, because they were all aware that I was from the hood.

While we sat and talked, I saw Ashley get up to get her food. I saw Dawson look at me and then look in the direction where I was looking to see what I was looking at. "Ohhh, snap!! Who is that?" He said as Thomas and Casper turned their heads in the same direction. "Oh Ashley, so that's who you guys are looking at." Thomas said. "You know her?" Dawson asked." Nah, I don't know her. But I heard about her. She's new. I think she transferred here so she could run track for us here. She's in my math class and that's what someone mentioned." Thomas said. "I-I-I a-a-actually u-u-used ta-to know her." I said as they all looked at me with surprise. "What?" "For real?" "Stop lying." They said one after the other while I shook my head yes. I told them that she wasn't the same as what she used to be and how she was acting all boujee now.

As I gave them a small backstory to how we met, I proceeded to tell them about what happened early today when I tried to talk to her. While telling them about how I got pushed down, Casper laughed continually while he kept saying that he wasn't laughing at me but at how Deon tried to act innocent after he pushed me. But I knew he was trying to clown me because, like I said, he wasn't really my friend. Dawson, being the slick mouth that he was said, "You should be glad that she didn't shake your hand, you probably would've fainted if she did." As he pretended to be me in the moment trying to shake her hand, leaning back while making his eyes roll into the back of his head to mimic me passing out. "Come on, guys. This is not funny, it's serious." Thomas said.

Eventually after we had all finished talking about the situation, lunch ended, and it was time to go back to class. 3:00pm came and it was time for me to go home. As I was leaving to get on the bus, I got a phone call from work. It was Mike, my supervisor. He informed me that one of my co-workers called off and couldn't make it to work and was asking me if I could come in. Knowing that I needed the money, I said yes and asked what time. Mike told me to get there by 4:00pm saying, "ok?" I said ok and literally as soon as I said ok, he said, "Good!" and hung up without thanking me for covering another employee's shift or showing any gratitude. Anyways, I headed back into the school lobby area to chill. Since I had about an hour of downtime and it only took me about seven or eight minutes to get to work, I decided to sit down and reflect on my first day.

After about twenty minutes of me thinking and pondering about what I would do with my life, I heard a voice shout, "Marlin!" I turned around in my chair and again to my surprise, it was Ashley. Now since it was the first day, tryouts for all the fall sports started today which included cheerleading. Although Ashley never cheered for a squad back when we were friends, I saw her in her practice cheer gear. As she approached me in the empty lobby, my body felt as if it went into a shock. The butterflies in my stomach felt like they were in rush hour and my heart felt like it shot up into my mouth. But I quickly calmed myself down.

Ashley: "Marlin, look, I know we was cool in the past, but that's the past. I don't want to seem phony and pretend like I never knew you, but I'm at another place in life right now. And I don't need people around me who ain't at that place right now…"

Me: "Wha-Wha-Wha-What ah-ah-ah-are you tryna…"

Ashley: "I'm saying that you're not at that place Marlin. I'm sorry to say it, but you not. I know that you liked me back then, and I'm sure you probably do now, but I only want men in life. Not boys…"

Me: "C'mon now Ashley, b-b-b-but…"

Ashley: "But nothing! It's nothing to talk about. Just accept it Marlin, we not friends, we not homies, we can't be cool. I'm sorry like… I just can't have you around me."

Me: "Wha-Wha-Wha-Why?"

Ashley: "Negro, I just told you why! Please don't make me have to point out the specifics cause your little feelings gone be hurt. I'm tryna' say it nice but obviously you ain't getting it. So let me stop sugar coating it... You're just... Not good enough for me. And I'm sorry if this breaks your heart, but that's just the reality of it. There's someone out there for you, who's on your level. But that's the way the world works. You can't have everything you see, that's why there's a price tag for the amount you have to pay to get it. I know we used to be friends and I'm thankful for the fun times that we had, but it's time for me to move on to... (slight pause) well, better things. And honestly, Marlin, you can't do anything for me to make me better. I'm sorry, and I don't think you're a bad person, I don't, you're just not on my level and people who aren't on my level always bring me down to theirs. So, do me a favor please and just don't speak when you see me. Ok?"

Me: (After Silence and deep breath)" ...Alright."

Ashley: (After fake smiling and walking away) "Thank you."

Wow, I was completely shocked. Appalled. This was not the same Ashley I knew before. This made me wonder what happened to her. Before, she was all sweet, nice, and innocent. Now, she was just blatantly rude. Disrespectful. And she looked as if she was a narcissist. And to be honest, what she said hurt. Like I said, I was different from everybody else. Being the kind of considerate and loving person I was, my feelings were more sensitive than most people. I know people would think that I'm trippin' over a girl, but it wasn't even about that. I was upset that someone who I had such good memories with over time decided that they don't want to have any association with me. I never even had a girlfriend, but with the way she cut me off it felt like I had gone through my first breakup.

But as I thought about it, she was right. I wasn't on her level. Whatever she did to be at the level that she was now, I wanted to know. But realistically, I wasn't good enough for her and I probably wouldn't ever be. I practically only had one real friend being here for my senior year while she was already making new friends on her first day at a new high school. Everybody wanted her and to be around her. She was desired and I wasn't. Man, what was I thinking, I should've known better, the way she was acting before she moved showed it all. I had to deal with it. I wasn't good enough and I wasn't going to ever be. I checked my phone, and it was almost time to start leaving for work. So, I packed my stuff and left.

Thankfully, I always kept my work clothes in a compartment in my bag, so I walked into work, changed, and clocked in. It was another busy day at work. I was running back and forth trying to complete tasks on time while the manager kept asking me to do other things. Fortunately, one of the pros of having a busy day was that it made the day go by quicker and before I knew it, my shift was almost over. It was about ten minutes to nine I finished cleaning up my last table and putting away all the waste from the tables. I took out the trash and finally my shift was over.

Usually when I would work late, Mama didn't want me to walk home after I would get off the public bus. Since she was usually at work herself, she couldn't pick me up. So, she would have one of her close friends who I called Auntie pay for an uber to get me home. Mama would pay her back half the amount that Auntie paid even though she would pay for the uber rides out of the goodness of her heart.

When I got home, it was 9:00pm. Julia was already sleep, and mama didn't make it home yet. I was exhausted mentally and physically. I didn't have much to eat after school except for some sample shish kabobs that I had at work. I was hungry, tired, and overall, done with today. I wanted to go to sleep and be done with it. I went to the refrigerator where I saw

74

that Mama had left some cooked pork chops and rice in a container for us, I put it on a plate, heated it up, and ate it. Afterwards, I went and got in the shower, changed into comfortable clothes, and got into my bed.

Before falling asleep, I thought about everything that had happened today: Taking long walks and transportation buses just to get to school, getting pushed down by Deon, getting rejected by Ashley, getting laughed at by my so called "friends", and rushing around at work tiring myself out. I thought to myself, "This can't be life. It has to be more to life than this." I was confused about why life had to be so hard for me. It looked as if it was a breeze for everyone else around me, but still a struggle for me. I know Deon or Ashley didn't have to go through this, and they deserved it now that I know the kind of people that they were.

I thought about English class, the class where I would have to see Ashley, the girl who I thought was my friend since the age of ten, ignore me every day for the rest of the year. And Deon, the guy who everybody loves, one of the most popular people in school and in the high school sports world, be my worst enemy. The class where I would have to give speeches...wait a minute, I forgot that I told myself that I was going to start working on my speech today. Well, that could wait, because at this point, I was too tired to do anything else.

By the way things were looking, it looked like it was going to be another rough year, even rougher than before now that I have Deon and Ashley to deal with. But I reminded myself of my goal, graduating high school, going to college, and finishing. That goal had the potential to get me to where I wanted to be, and how rewarding it would be if I accomplished it. With this in mind, I felt a little bit better. But doubt still clouded my mind. With all these oppositions and distractions, my goal could easily fade away. So, I held on to this goal in my mind with everything I had.

Hopefully it wasn't too late to try and start on a finished project, because senior year is the year where most students get to relax, kick their feet up, and chill as their grades and college choices are already set in place. But I still had to grind for mine. So I went to bed that night falling asleep to sirens, the music sounds of the streets.

CHAPTER 5: RISING TURMOIL

I woke up about 8:00am on Saturday which meant that I would have to start getting ready for work soon. Usually on Saturday's I worked at noon and would get off late. Considering the time that it would take for me to get to work, my Saturdays were full. I got up and out of bed and did my normal morning routine getting myself washed up. After washing up, I headed into the kitchen where Mama and Julia were talking. "Girl, stop playing and drink that smoothie, it's good for you." I heard Mama saying to Julia. "But it's green, and it got carrots in it." Julia said as I walked in. "Girl if you don't…look, watch me, all you gotta' do is…hey, Marlin!" Mama said when she saw me walk into the kitchen, after trying to get Julia to drink her smoothie. Julia put down her smoothie and ran over to hug me.

"Wha-Wha-Wha-What, y'all ma-ma-must be in a good mu-mu-mood today." I said responding to their attention. "Yea, you know Julia got invited to a tournament today. It starts at three. That's why I keep telling her to drink her smoothie."

77

Mama stated while looking at Julia playfully. Julia, after staring at Mama for a while, finally took a sip of her smoothie and made a sour face. "It tastes like…a water potato salad." Julia said with a disgusted face, chewing on the drinkable smoothie. "Girl…!" Mama shouted after she screamed in laughter. "Oh, and Marlin, I can drop you off at work today." She added.

Typically, Mama couldn't take me to work because she had to work. But since today was one of her off days and she was in a good mood; she was willing to. Although she was usually reluctant to do so because she was on a budget and didn't want to burn up gas money. After I finished getting ready it was 11:35am, so Mama and I left while Julia stayed home by herself. When Mama was taking me to work, she asked about the colleges that I had in mind and my potential major. It had only been two weeks since my first day of school, so I didn't really have an idea of what college or career path I would choose. However, I didn't want to say that I had no idea. But since I did have this passion for speaking and interacting with others to bring about a positive change, I thought of a therapist. I decided that that's what I would tell Mama, that I wanted to be a therapist. Although I knew nothing about what education that I would need to have, how many years of school that I would need, where I could apply to be a therapist if I did go to college, or how I would even do as therapist if I was even fortunate enough to become one. But I knew that this would please Mama's ears because it was something professional and would allow me to make good money.

After briefly pausing, I finally proceeded to tell her that I wanted to be a therapist. "Oh, really?! Ok, I got me a lil therapist sitting next to me." She replied with a surprised voice, appearing to be impressed and placing her hand on her chest. "But you know you gone have to go to school for that and probably need a master's degree." She added. In response, I said, "Ye-Ye-Ye-Yea, I-I-I know." "Yea, and you know too though that school is expensive, and I don't have the money for you to go to a university or even a junior college. So, you'll have to take out some loans, but you definitely gone need to find a way to get some scholarships if you want to go to college. Grandma might be able to help you, but she is only going to be able to do so much. And you're gonna' have to bring your grades up too." Mama added while transitioning into a more concerned and serious tone.

Now I never actually planned to be a therapist, or anything related to it. I never planned anything big for my life as I always felt that whatever I did wasn't enough to get me to where I wanted to be. I was just saying this to make Mama feel that I was on to something great, when, I wasn't even sure myself. But now that I mentioned it, being a therapist didn't even sound like such a bad idea. One, it would allow me to make enough money to move out of the hood and make it out, two, it would be a professional career that I was seeking for, three, it would allow me to live out my passion of speaking to help others, and four... Oh, wait a minute, speaking.

I failed to realize that all therapists would have to conversate with their clients to help them properly. Which in my case would be a major struggle and may even disqualify me from doing the job because of my stuttering. In addition, I knew that I would have to get better in my communication skills and in my English. English, hold on, wait a minute... Another minute. It's been two weeks of school and I still haven't even started on my speech for English class that I said I was going to start on the first day of school. Well, at least I still had two more weeks to figure it out, but these past two weeks went by so fast especially since I had to work and was busy trying to keep my grades up in my other classes. But this, to me, was already a bad sign. As I continued to unintentionally procrastinate my speech that was worth a large portion of my grade due to all my other issues in life. But I still decided to keep the idea of becoming a therapist in my mind and stick to it even though I felt that it was unlikely.

Finally, after about a twenty-minute ride, I arrived at work. Mama dropped me off and told me that she'll have her friend, which I called Auntie, get an uber for me to get back home. So, I thanked my mom for driving me to work and said goodbye. I walked into work and clocked in. As I walked into the room where all the cleaning supplies were to get situated, I saw Mike, standing with Bruno. Bruno was a new employee who started two weeks ago. Over the past two weeks, Bruno had worked in the mornings, but had apparently gotten moved around to different shifts. Today was my turn to work with him.

"Marlin, this is Bruno, I want you to work with him since he's kind of new and you've been here for a while. Maybe you can teach him a few things." Mike said before he walked out of the room. Even though I knew who Bruno was, I never met him. So, I came over to Bruno, nodding my head at him, and reaching out my hand so he can shake it. Bruno looked, quickly grabbed the tips of my fingers with his hand, pulled them down, and went on his way. I wasn't sure whether that was supposed to be him shaking my hand or a sign to me that he didn't like me. Either way, I didn't have time to try and figure it out as I was just trying to get the day over with.

As I started to clean off the tables, I noticed some eyes staring at me. After ignoring it, I finally looked up and it was Bruno watching me from afar. I continued to ignore him and went about doing my job alternating between duties. After a few minutes, I went into the back to go get some water when the manager Mike approached me. "What is this!?" He asked holding a napkin with chicken bones in it. I tried to respond by saying, "Tha-tha-tha-tha-tha-that's nah-na-not eh...", but Mike interrupted and exclaimed, "Check all the tables before you leave them next time! If it wasn't for Bruno, these chicken wing bones would've stayed on the table!"

Now it made sense why Bruno was watching so hard while I was cleaning, he wanted to see me make a mistake to correct it. But he couldn't correct any of my mistakes if he didn't see me make one. Typically, after I picked up all the trash from the tables and wiped them down, I'd look back and check for anything I missed. Of course, I wasn't perfect so there were times when I checked, saw something, and removed it from the tables before the customers sat down. All the while, Bruno was watching, waiting for me to make a mistake so he could play tattle tale. But I had a weird feeling about Bruno. I felt that he was a weird person but not just weird in a sense of how he acted, but I felt a weird vibe from him. I sensed something negative about him. Like he was up to something against me and that explains why he "shook" my hand the way that he did.

How would Mike have known to blame me for the chicken bones on the table? Unless Bruno would have told him. I mean, it could've been a customer. So, I decided to keep a close eye on him as he did me. Luckily for Bruno, he was in a safe environment because if he would've pulled this stunt back where I lived, he would've run into some big problems.

Eventually, later in my shift, it was time for me to go on lunch. Since I worked at a restaurant, there was a wide variety of meals that I could choose from. But the problem was that they were all expensive. Since I didn't get any benefits because I wasn't a manager or a chef, I was limited in the meals that I would get the benefit from in the restaurant. So, I just got some nachos from the appetizers menu which were about ten dollars. Way overpriced for the amount that I got, but it was the most affordable thing for me to eat with the forty dollars that I had left to spend.

Afterwards, I finished eating and got back to work. Then, Mike comes up to me again and starts complaining about a dirty napkin that Bruno found in the break room. I knew already that Mike didn't like me, but it also became evident to me that Bruno was plotting against me. Instead of being mature and throwing it away, this boy decides to tell the manager that I left a dirty napkin on the table. Since Mike didn't like me, he entertained Bruno's childish antics. Great, now I had enemies at work and at school, even when minding my own business.

As my shift was ending, I finally had some down time as I was finishing up my duties making sure everything was in its proper place being neat and clean with proper maintenance before I left. Then, I saw Bruno who was still on the clock, sitting down hiding from the managers as we were slowing down. This hinted to me that during the last part of my shift, he was absent allowing me to do all the work. After everything that I had went through today because of Bruno, I was fed up with it. So, I decided to confront him despite how he would feel about it.

I approached him being very direct, straightforward, and bold, stating loud and clearly, "A-A-A-Aye, aye Bruh-Bruh-Bruh-Bruh-Bruno!" as he turned his head quickly towards me, paying attention to me. "Wha-Wha-Wha-Wha-Wha-What's yo problem ma-ma-man. What?" I asked once I had his attention. I wasn't trying to make a scene and believe it or not I didn't feel like doing this, but I knew that at some point I had to confront him about his attitude. I had to confront him because if he continued to watch me for every little detail all the time to find a mistake, it would lead to me going off on him or cause me to lose this job. Even though I hated this job since I first started, I didn't want to get fired because of this boy tattle tailing on me every shift. Sadly, I needed this job because it was my only source of income that put money in my pocket. Although it was just pocket change and most of it was income that we all depended on to keep the house up and running at home. To make it worse, it didn't appear that I could get any other source of income besides this job any time soon since I always struggled to find a new job that would hire me.

After I confronted Bruno, he looked at me like he was shocked with a blank expression on his face and then finally said, "You, you too complicated." Uh, what? I thought to myself. Was he trying to say that I'm complicated? "A-A-A-A All I n-n-n-know is, yu-yu-you tried to ma-ma-make me look bad t-t-to the manager. Like why bruh?". Bruno replied saying, "I work hard. Harder than you. And you, you don't get work done right. So, I get it done for you, the right way." When he said this, I saw Mike looked over at us and walked over to us. "Guys, what's the problem?" He asked.

That's when I told Mike about how I saw Bruno sitting down chilling while he was still on the clock when we had fifteen minutes left to go and that I had to do all the work at the end of my shift because of it. "Well Bruno is still new, and his shift started before yours did and he leaves after you. So that's fine that he's taking a break right now." Mike responded. "Are you kidding me?" I thought to myself. Bruno wasn't some angel, but he was being treated like the savior of the restaurant and apparently, I was seen as the one who the restaurant needed saving from.

"I don't think he like me." Bruno said to Mike while pointing to me. "That's ok, Bruno. We're all family here. Marlin, I want you to be an example to Bruno. If you see him doing something that he's not supposed to, don't get upset and yell, just teach him." At this point, I didn't even respond. What about all the times that I messed up and Mike yelled at me instead of being a teacher? I was over it, I stared at Bruno as he got up and it seemed like he was ready to get back to work because Mike was there. Even though he appeared to have no intentions of getting back to work before Mike came over.

I went outside to wait for my uber ride that Mama said Auntie paid for. A few minutes later, I got a phone call from her. She told me that the driver would take a little longer than the original estimated time. She said it would only take an extra ten minutes until I could be picked up. So, I waited. The ten minutes went by and nothing. Another ten minutes went by and still nothing. After that I started to get curious about where the uber was, so I called Auntie. The phone rang, and rang, and rang. And then finally... Her voicemail pops up telling me to leave a message. So, I decided to call her again after a few minutes to see if she would pick up thinking that she may have been away from the phone at the time. And it went to her voicemail again.

That's when I started to get a slight feeling of panic because I started to feel stranded with no way to get home. I got my phone and started to call Mama. After a few rings, she picked up and I told her about what was happening, and that Auntie wasn't answering her phone. So, she told me to hold on so she could try and get a hold of her but there was still no pickup from Auntie. Mama and I both started to worry as to how I was going to get home because Mama was still at work. No uber had showed up after about twenty-five minutes and nobody was getting off from their shift who would possibly be able to take mc home.

Then as I was on the phone with Mama, I saw a car pull up and it was Thomas. "Aye Marlin, need a ride?" He shouted out of his car window. And after I asked Mama about Thomas dropping me off, she approved of it and gave me the ok to get in. When I got into the car, Thomas and I greeted each other with our handshake and started to talk as he drove off.

Thomas: "Yo bro, what's good. Don't you usually take an uber home from work or something?"

Me: "Ye-Ye-Yea, but it di-di-d-didn't show up this ta-ta-time."

Thomas: "What? That's crazy, man. Good thing I saw you when I did. Oh yea, you can just tell me where to go from here. What's new man? How was work?"

Me: "Pssshhh… Don't e-e-e-even mention it b-b-b-b-b-bruh. I-I-I-It's this new g-g-guy a-a-at work and he-he been sni-sni-snitching on me. He t-t-tells the manager e-e-everything I do ra-ra-ra-wrong."

Thomas: "Awe man I know that's annoying. What kind of stuff does he tell on you about?"

Me: "P-P-P-P-Petty stuff. Like I wa-wa-was eating and I ha-ha-had a napkin that I left i-i-in the break room awe-awe-on a table and the new g-g-g-g-g-guy tells the manger."

Thomas: "Dang, that's terrible."

(As I was directed Thomas closer to my neighborhood.)

Thomas: "Whooaa… You live in this area?"

Me: "Ye-Ye-Yea man, and this isn't e-e-e-even a-a-all the way to where I live. I s-s-s-s-somet-t-times t-t-t-take the bus and then walk home after that."

Thomas: "I mean, this area isn't too bad but it's pretty different from where I live. But I don't know man, to be honest bro, I'm a little scared to take you all the way to your house in your neighborhood especially with all the stories you've told me about in the past."

Me: "Na-na-na-na-nah bro, ih-ih-ih-ih-it's cool. You p-p-p-probably wouldn't want to go a-a-around there a-a-a-anyways since you driving this car and s-s-s-since you are uh… Weh-Well…"

Thomas: "White?"

Me: "Yea. Aye, j-j-j-j-just dra-dra-dra-drop m-m-m-me off at that bus stop down there bro and I-I-I-I-I-I'll be good. Thanks m-m-m-man. Preciate ih-ih-ih-it."

Thomas: "Alright man."

Me: "Yea (After getting to the bus stop while getting out of his car.) Alright th-th-th-th-thanks bro, I appreciate it."

Thomas: "Alright, I'll see you later at school bro."

After I got out of Thomas' car waiting at the bus stop, I finally got on the south bus instead of the north that I would normally take to get to the school bus stop. At this point it was already past nine and I remembered how Mama would always be nervous about me walking around our neighborhood late at night. I thought about calling her, but I didn't want her to waste gas by picking me up when I could casually walk home. Plus, I liked to ponder so walking would allow me to have time to do that.

I thought about "Auntie", who was just a close friend of Mama, supposedly calling a uber to pick me up. I wondered if she knew it was going to take even longer than the time that she said that it would take to get there or if she lied. I wondered if she was really away from the phone when her voicemail went off when Mama and I had called her, or if she just didn't answer on purpose. But either way, this raised a major red flag in my mind because not only did my uber not show up in timely fashion, but Auntie didn't even answer the phone. Not once but twice and she didn't even bother to call either of us back after the missed calls.

This told me that she wasn't completely reliable and made me doubt whether I could trust her in the future. But if I couldn't trust her, then who could I trust to be consistent to get me home or at least get me to the bus stop so I could walk home? I knew that I could trust Mama if she was in the position to be able to take me back and forth to work each time but, she wasn't. She was always busy at work, and she often didn't want to burn the gas money, but I didn't want her to do that either when it wasn't necessary. How was I going to get back and forth to work to the only place where I was able to make money now? I didn't want to bother Thomas all the time. I knew it would be too much walking for me to get to the bus stops which would take up even more of my little time that I had to use for studying. That meant I wouldn't do as well in school this year as I planned to accomplish my goal. I wanted to give my all and do the best that I could.

Right as I was thinking this and walking, I saw this pimped out Dodge Charger pull up ahead of me, with rims and everything. As I continued my way home while moving toward the vehicle, I heard one of the guys in the car yell, "AYE! AYE LIL' BRO!" I looked into the car and saw three young black men with white t-shirts playing gangster rap. Being from the hood I was no stranger to these kinds of encounters. But what separated this encounter was that these guys looked serious. Usually in these situations, people would only do this to get a reaction. But this time, these guys looked like they did it with a purpose and wanted my undivided attention as I saw the driver use his head to signal me to come over.

This left me in a mini mental crisis. I remember Mama drilling me when I was younger about not having interactions with people who appeared to be in gangs or looked mischievous. But by the way that they were looking at me, I thought that if I ignored them then it would cause a worse issue. On the other hand, if I did talk to them, I had a bad feeling that it would lead to something bad. So, I quickly weighed my options and figured that if I just go over to see what they wanted and not jump to conclusions, that it wouldn't be as bad as ignoring them and making them get angry which could bring more controversy.

I walked over to their car not getting too close being very aware and cautious of my surroundings.

Driver: "Aye lil bro, you got a dollar or sum'?"

Me: (Shaking my head no.) "I'm ba-ba-ba-ba-ba-ba-b-b-broke."

Passenger 1: (Laughing.) "He said, 'I'm broke." (More Laughing.)

Driver: "Nah, we ain't need no money man, we just wanna see if you had sum or not. But since you mention it, we starting our own group with dancin' entertainment stuff, feel me? And we could use sum body that roll wit' us to make our videos in a better way. We ah pay you for it, feel me. But for real doe we tryna make it out and start our own."

Me: (Blank Stare)

Passenger 1: "What he sayin' is, he want you to be our new camera man and special effects editor. See cus', my boy inna back he dance too, but he can't never dance with us because he be recording and filming us and doin' stuff like dat. But if you record for us, he can dance with us, you edit it, and it ah be mo raw, ya feel me?"

Driver: "You can record and stuff?"

Me: "I ma-ma-mean, I-I-I na-na-know i-i-i-it a-a-ain't that h-h-h-h-h-hard. But…"

Driver: "And listen bruh, we ain't no gang or nun like that bro, we just tryna make it out the hood, for real, through this stuff. I promise, we ain't never bother no body, we don't want no trouble, we about that money. And really, we all just met not too long ago, feel me? But we tryna expand our brand too. But we don't let just anybody join our circle you feel me? So, you better get on board while you still can if you tired of being broke. I see sum in you lil homie, sum big. That's why you ah be even more raw wit' us, feel me? What? You don't wanna make money like this? (Flashes some money) C'mon man we all family?"

Me: (Silence.)

Driver: "Aye but think about it bro. But my name Jahmoni, but you can call me Moni. But we gon.'" (Hands me a business card.)

Me: "A-A-A-Alright, I'm Marlin."

Driver: "Aight Marlin but think about it doe." (Drives away.)

I continued to walk home and thought about what happened. As much as I didn't want to admit it, this "opportunity" didn't seem that bad. Considering I was desperate to make some money being in the situation that I was in, my mind started to consider it. But wait a minute, there was no way in the world that Mama would ever let me join a "group" like this especially since she didn't know them. I didn't even know them. But it was something about Jahmoni, the driver, that was persuasive. I wasn't sure what it was, but he seemed cool to be around although he was still a stranger to me.

Then suddenly, as I was about to approach the block that my house was on, I heard loud sounds of gun shots from a nearby block. "BANG! BANG! BANG! DOOF! DOOF!" When I heard this, I automatically sprinted down the block the whole way until I got to my home where I hurriedly used my key to get through the front gate, went through the apartment doors, and banged on our door in panic and shock although I had my key to open it. Mama, knowing it was me through the peephole, quickly opened the door, pushed me inside, closed the door, and locked it.

"I WAS CALLING YOU ON YO PHONE, MARLIN! WHAT TOOK YOU SO LONG?!" Mama asked with major concern. "I-I-I-I-I h-h-h-h-had t-t-t-to walk ha-ha-ha-ha-home from that bus stop I-I-I-I-I take to s-s-s-school." I responded out of breath, terrified, and flustered. "You walked? Why didn't you just ask me, and I woulda came and picked you up? What? That other boy who was supposed to drive you home was too scared to come over here?" I looked at her still in slight shock over what just happened. Julia came from out of her room and ran to me and gave me a hug to show that she was also worried.

"Marlin, I know that Auntie flaked on us, and I would usually be working right now, but it's past 8pm, and you know that's when the streets really start getting dangerous. And you know that's when them gangbanging boys be out there. You didn't speak to none of them, did you?" Mama asked while ranting at me. "Nah Ma, I-I-I-I-I'm good, I-I-I ju-ju-ju-just wanna l-l-l-lay down. It's b-b-b-been a long d-d-d-day." I responded while walking towards the bathroom to take a shower and lay down.

Then, finally once I laid down in my room, Julia came in and asked, "Marlin, you ok?" "Y-y-yea, I'm good. I'm t-t-t-t-tryna' go to sleep r-r-right now so…" I said as she looked at me while I turned to the other side and pulled the covers over myself even more. Without saying anything she left the room. And in no time, I was fast asleep.

I woke up early the next day, it was Sunday morning. We didn't usually go to church on Sundays because Mama would always have to work. So, our Sundays were spent inside usually if I didn't have to work. I went into the bathroom where I saw Mama in the mirror getting ready to go to her second job as a cashier at a grocery store.

"H-h-h-hey Ma." I spoke. "Hey, son." She responded. "We might have to find another way for you to get home from work." She said. "Cause your Auntie starting to act funny now. I finally was able to get a hold of her last night when you went to sleep. And she talm' bout, *'Oh, it's none of my business to get him a ride. I can't give him a ride all the time. Why can't you give him a ride?'* She continued while rolling her eyes. "And then she gone say that she just forgot. You ain't forget you just ain't pay for it and then gone lie to you talm bout' *'Oh it was just late.'* Like girl, I'm reimbursing you for it, even though it's not all at once, you still getting something back for it. And then you said that you'll do it to help us out. But now you mean to tell me that you done changed your mind, but you call yourself my sister? Psshh... What a joke." She finally added shaking her head after fixing up her hair.

As she headed for the front door, she told me not to worry about it as she promised to find a way for me to get home without having to walk through the streets at night. But really, as much as I wanted to believe Mama, I knew that she herself was unsure about how to do it. Now I felt worried about how I was going to get home safely. Then, a little later after Mama left, I heard my phone ring. I looked at it and saw that it was grandma calling.

Me: "H-h-h-h-hey, G-g-g-gra-gra-gra-gra-grandma."

Grandma: "Hey baby (Coughs hard.) Woo... How you been?"

Me: "I-I-I-I-I b-b-b-been good. Y-y-y-you ok? You s-s-s-sound sick."

Grandma: "Yea I'm ok baby. So, what's going on over there. How's everybody.

Me: We're g-g-g-good.

(Julia hears us talking and comes to the phone.)

Julia: "HEY GRANDMA!"

Grandma: "Hey honey, how you doin'?"

Julia: "I'm good."

Me: "I-I-I-I h-h-h-had to w-w-w-walk home fr-f-f-f-from work y-y-yesterday and then I heard g-g-g-gun shots so I instantly ga-g-g-g-got to running to get back ha-h-h-home."

Grandma: "Oh my goodness, what happened I thought somebody brings you home from work?"

Me: "Not this t-t-t-t-t-time, m-m-m-my Auntie t-t-t-told Mama that she 'f-f-f-f-f-forgot' t-t-t-to pay but she told m-m-m-me that the uber w-w-w-w-would be late when in reality, i-i-i-it never showed uh-uh-uh-up."

Grandma: "Mmmm…that's a shame. But this is what I'll do, tell your mother to call me and send me the link for that uber thing. I don't have too much money, but I don't wanna see you out here like that. Also, text me the days and times that you work ahead of time, so I know how to schedule it for you. Can you do that for me?"

Me: "Th-th-th-thank you Grandma. I-I-I-I-It means a lot. Oh y-y-y-yea, and I forgot to tell you th-th-th-th-th-that I think I know what I want to be a-a-after High-School."

Grandma: "Ooohh, go head tell it to me baby."

Me: "I-I-I-I decided th-th-th-th-th-that I-I-I-I-I w-wu-want to be a therapist."

Grandma: "Oooh, gone head baby! Now that's what I'm talking about. You gone be a educated young black man. Now that's not gone be easy now, you got to work. But I believe in you. Like I always say to you, God got some big things in store for you. You just wait and see. Big things!" (More coughing) "Whew, baby that was a rough one. But what you and your little sister got planned for the rest of the day over there?"

Me: "W-w-w-w-well, I-I-I-I-I know I got a la-la-la-lot of homework left to do. And its p-p-p-probably going t-t-t-to take a-a-a-all day for me to finish it b-b-b-because algebra and ph-ph-physics ain't easy for me and J-J-J-Julia is probably just g-g-gonna' relax since she had a tournament yesterday so…"

Grandma: "Oh ok, well since you have homework that you need to get done, imma let you go about your day then. But I'm praying for you sweetheart. Hold on and hang on in their baby, because that value is about to come outta you. Everything you've gone through is going to start making sense once you see what God is about to do in your life."

Me: "O-o-o-ok Gra-gra-grandma, I appreciate that. I-I-I-I'm praying for you too."

Grandma: "Alright bye-bye, talk to you later sweetheart."

Me: "Alright bye-bye."

I finally got off the phone with Grandma and headed back into my room so that I could start on my homework. Since it was still early, I figured I'd just sit on my phone and browse the internet a little bit before I start since I had the whole day pretty much to myself. As I got on my phone and started scrolling through it, I saw the business card that Jahmoni had given me when he approached me. On the bottom were his social media usernames so I decided to check him out on YouTube. When I saw that the name of his group come up on the internet, I was taken by surprise. I saw that each of his videos raked in tens of thousands of views. So, I clicked on one of them and it was exactly how he described it to me in the car. Two men in a house dancing to popular rap songs while the camera moved around and switched to different angles.

I quickly scrolled to the comment section and saw how everybody talked about how their dances were "lit" how they were all super talented, and how they had a bright future ahead of them if they continued to do what they did. This threw all the skepticism that I had about them out of the window. It caused me to want to learn more about them and made me start to consider joining in with them even more.

I exited out from YouTube to see what was new on my social media feed. Before I even got into any heavy scrolling, I saw a post by an official sports page that said, "TOP 10 HIGH SCHOOL WIDE RECEIVERS IN ILLINOIS IN THEIR SENIOR SEASON" tagging the wide receivers who were said to be the top ten. Among them, at number five, was Deon. So, I clicked on Deon's username and started to scroll on his page as I quickly came to a picture of him out with friends at an upscale restaurant. In the comment section below the photo, I saw someone with the name "Ash" as their username post, "You didn't leave any for me?" with a sad face emoji.

Instantly, I already knew it was Ashley. So, I clicked on her username which bought me to her page. Immediately, I saw pictures of her running track and clips of her workout routines. As I continued to scroll, I saw a video that was posted of Ashley sprinting in a track meet. When I clicked play, I saw how she immediately got out to a quick lead and dominated the entire race being the only one in the picture before crossing the finish line. After seeing this, it made sense why Ashley felt like she was way above me. I also saw that she had multiple scholarship offers, interviews, and a large following social media.

Suddenly, I could feel that feeling of worry, frustration, and low self-worth that started to cloud over me because of all the things I that was currently seeing and experiencing that were now starting to become overbearing. Everything. From Bruno, Mike, and my work situation, always having to deal with Mike's domineering personality, his rude treatment towards me, and his little care for me as a human. To now having to deal with Bruno's sneaky, antics and his conflicting attitude which seemed to only be targeted towards me. From always having to work myself until I feel like I can't anymore for minimum wage. Just to keep the house up and running because I felt that if I ever quit or got fired, the rent wouldn't get paid, or we would have to go without our essentials. To always working in fear. Being fearful thinking that if I lost this opportunity at this job, there would be a regression in my household, even though it was a job that I hated.

From not having a sure way to get home from work because of a lying, dishonest, unreliable, and inconsistent "friend" of the family who suddenly decides to turn her back on us for no apparent reason. Knowing that were struggling as a family despite our hard work. To debating whether I should associate myself with people who could either help or hurt me.

From living in a dangerous environment where almost anything goes. Where people get away with things that leave others traumatized. And being forced to be in the middle of it no matter how much I tried to isolate myself from it. To always having to live in constantly alert, precaution, nervousness, anxiety, and panic because of the fear that I could become victim to gun violence or police brutality being a young black boy from the ghetto.

All while watching everybody else's life flourish, thrive, and evolve into great things through entertainment and academics but seeing my life continue to dry up because I had no real talent, gifts, skills, or special abilities to work with. In addition to seeing my peers, who set themselves as my enemies for no other reason than to make me feel worse about myself, get blessed in my face while I suffered.

All these things mentioned are things that I continued to see and experience that kept on rising and multiplying themselves into more problems. It's like my life was becoming filled with turmoil, turmoil that sought out my very life. The ONLY thing at this point that really kept me going was my big dream that I had a small chance of accomplishing. And honestly, if it wasn't for this new goal that I hoped to achieve, I don't know how I would have even made it this far. I was running out of options, hope, and faith. Stability, inner peace and fulfillment, happiness, and confidence seemed to be running away from me while turmoil seemed to be the only thing that was running to me.

I needed God to come through with something special. And even though I was far from perfect, didn't pray or read the bible as much as I should have, because I was always busy doing the things that needed to be done so my family and I could survive, I still did my best to have a relationship with God and trust Him.

Even after years of seeking Jesus early in my childhood, struggling to have faith because of things that had happened in the past, and not seeing things that I prayed for come to past when I wanted them to, I told myself that I still wouldn't give up on God. I wouldn't give up on Jesus just yet because I wanted to show Him that I was remaining strong through it all. But realistically, I knew that I couldn't remain strong much longer being in the position that I was in.

But I believed that there was still a chance that He could turn things around, help me with academics in school, and grant me the intelligence that I needed to do well this year so I could go to college and succeed. But with all the rising turmoil I saw and experienced, it made me question if God was really on my side. Or if God, the most powerful, dominant, and decisive being in the universe, was against me.

CHAPTER 6: CLIMAX

About a week had went by and it was time to start the week off fresh on a Monday morning. I had arrived at school, and it was about time that I start heading to my English class. I went to my locker to go put some things in there when I saw Ashley and Jack nearby. They both stood across from each other as they held hands pecking on the lips before they came together for a hug. After I walked into the class, I saw Ashley walk in while one of the female students in the class said, "Ooooh, girl I saw you out there with your man." "Yea girl, he took me out yesterday and asked me out. I'm just like sitting there like, 'Boy you shoulda' asked me sooner, with your fine white chocolate self.'" Ashley said with laughter and a huge smile on her face.

"Oh Deon, I texted you about the homework for our Statistics class, but you didn't respond." Ashley said to Deon as soon as he walked in the class. "Oh, my bad. I must've been working out when you texted me." Deon said as he stopped to check his phone. "What? Why did you send me a kiss emoji after it?" He added. "Oh, I did? Awe, my fault. I meant to send that to Jack. For real, like I'm so serious." Ashley responded smiling at Deon while he smiled back at her saying, "Oh ok.", looking at her up and down before walking to his seat. "Alright class! Sorry I'm late but the traffic was terrible." Mr. Wysol said upon walking in the classroom.

As class started, Mr. Wysol began to talk about the importance of staying focused on what we had to do for school. He mentioned about how he knows that many of us have other hobbies besides school and how we shouldn't let these hobbies interfere with our schoolwork. He began to stress how hard it was to get a decent job without a solid high school GPA and college education. Using scare tactics, he said, "And without a college degree or having a post high school education, you'll probably end up working at a fast-food restaurant for most of your life. And you don't want that do you? So please do yourselves a favor stay in school, finish, do well, and make it a priority in your life. Because if you don't, you might end up working some dead-end job that you hate for most of your life and be ashamed of it."

After he said this, reality hit me even harder, and I began to fear even more for my future. Because I knew that this was the exact position that I was in. And although I still had the rest of this year to try and help it, I thought about the more than likely chance of me poorly doing this year and ending up working at my current job or some other low-end job. With the teacher making this statement, I felt a sense of nervousness, anxiousness, and worry rising within me that would reoccur every time I thought about my future. No matter how I tried to deal with it, it wouldn't be suppressed. Then, he reminded us again that our speeches were going to be performed this Friday. Great. I picked out the poetic speech that I wanted but I had only looked at it a few times and didn't remember any of it. So, I knew that I had to put in work this week and get it done.

After this quick lecture, the teacher proceeded to say, "Oh, and I hope you guys read the chapter in your books over the weekend, because as I promised, we will have a class group discussion. So, I'll divide you into groups. When I finish calling out all the names you can get with your groups. Group 1: Marlin, Ashley, and Deon..." "C'mon man." I thought to myself as the teacher called out the groups. I practically had to be in the same group with two of my enemies. After the teacher called out all the groups, everyone started to get their things together and switch seats to sit next to their group.

I moved my belongings to where Deon and Ashley were sitting. They ignored me as I sat down but started talking to each other.

Deon: "Wait, Ashley did you read the chapter?"

Ashley: "I read part of it, did you?"

Deon: "I got like four or five pages left that I didn't finish. But anyway, wassup with you and Jack?"

Ashley: "Oh Jack? That's bae now. He is just so sweet, like yesterday he took me out and bought me food. Then he took me to this candy shop and bought me some dessert and flowers and then he asked me to be his girl." (Smiling and tilting head to the side.)

Deon: "Oh, word? That's wassup. So, what's new with you bugly?"

Ashley: (Giggling.) "Deon…"

Me: (Looking up.) "Who? M-m-m-m-m-me?"

Deon: (Laughing.) "Yea you."

Me: "L-l-l-l-look, b-b-b-bro you n-n-not j-j-j-ju-ju-just g-g-g-g…"

Deon: (More Laughing.)

Ashley: (Laughing covering her mouth.)

Me: (Quickly and aggressively standing up in anger.) "BOY, I-I-I-IF Y-Y-Y-YOU KEEP ON TALKIN, I SWEAR I'M GONE…!!!"

(Students in class look, items fall of desk, desk moves.)

Mr. Wysol: "Whoa! Whoa! Whoa! What's going on guys? (After silence, and staring) "Marlin, step outside please."

Me: (Calms down. Walks outside with teacher.)

Mr. Wysol: "Marlin, what seems to be the problem?"

Me: "Deon. He's the p-p-p-p-problem. H-h-h-he always t-t-t-trying to m-m-m-make f-f-f-fun of m-m-m-me."

Mr. Wysol: "Deon? What? What did he do?"

Me: "He c-c-c-c-called me a-a-a-out of m-m-my name."

Mr. Wysol: "Ok, I'll talk to him. But you need to control your emotions. If you need me to put you in another group that's fine but it's only ten more minutes left and I'm sure you can handle that. Alright? Ready to go back in?"

Me: Ok. (Walks back into class with teacher.)

I walked back in as everyone looked at me and stared. I came and sat back down in my seat with the teacher telling us that we had about ten minutes left to get our thoughts together.

Deon and Ashley both looked at me like they were holding in laughter when I walked in, and I knew exactly why. When Ashley and I used to be friends, the nickname that I was often referred to as was ugly-bugly. I remember when Ashley would hear others call me this, she would come to my defense saying that no one could call me bugly or say that I looked like a bug when they were the ones bugging me about how I looked.

But now it was evident that she was now sharing that old nickname with others and using it against me. It was obvious to me that Deon had learned of the term bugly from Ashley and was now using it to make fun of me. Deon didn't even know who I was before this year, so this was the only way that he could have found out.

Before I knew it, the teacher bought the group discussion to an end, and it was time to share what we had discussed in our groups. "So, group 1, what are some of the things that stood out to you as you read the chapter?" Mr. Wysol asked. Deon stated a quote that came from the chapter and gave his opinion as Ashley followed up on what he said. I remained quiet as I didn't really get a chance to hear what Deon and Ashley were saying about the book while I had left the room. "Marlin, do you have anything that you would like to add?" Mr. Wysol asked. I shook my head no. "Did you even read the chapter?" He asked. I looked down at the ground and quietly responded no. Mr. Wysol responded, "Well, that's going to hurt your grade but ok, group 2?", after sighing, raising his eyebrows, and shaking his head in disappointment while writing on what appeared to be a grade sheet.

As all the other groups shared their thoughts and ideas, I thought about this class. Last week I remembered we had a pop-quiz and I recently found out that I had failed it. Although it was only about three questions and was one out of the twenty quizzes we would probably have, I considered this to be strike one. It was already a bad start to this class. Now that I saw how Mr. Wysol reacted when he found out that I didn't read, I knew that he would put me as a non-participant of the group which could lead to me receiving a zero for this assignment, strike two. Now, my third and final possibility of getting a strike was coming up this week. We all know the rules, three strikes, and you're out. I was on my last chance before a strike out, and considering that I had been somewhat practicing, but still didn't remember any of my speech, it was likely that I could strike out, for good. Meaning that my grade for this class, which was mandatory for graduation, would be at such a low point that it would be hard to come back from.

After the bell rung, Mr. Wysol reminded us again about our speeches and stated that if we didn't know any part of it by now that we could be in danger of doing poorly. He said he would grade us rather strictly since he was constantly reminding us to practice since the beginning of school. I walked into the hallway where I saw Jack nearby waiting for Ashley. When she came out, I saw the two grab each other's hands as I saw Deon approach his girlfriend Freida giving her a couple of pecks on the lips. I turned my head away and continued to go about the rest of my day.

Eventually, after more labor on schoolwork, it came time for lunch. I went and got my usual bag of chips and drink and sat down at the lunch table with Thomas. After a few minutes, Dawson and Casper came and sat down with us.

Dawson: "Yo, I went to get in line, and I saw the funniest thing."

Thomas: "What?"

Dawson: "It was this girl who got almost everything, snacks and toppings in the line, but didn't even have enough money to pay for it."

Casper: (Outbursts in laughter.)

Thomas: "What's so funny about that?"

Dawson: "The fact that she tried to buy all that stuff but couldn't pay for it."

Thomas: "Anyways I have something to show you guys. (Goes in backpack, pulls out paper.) Look."

Casper: "Awe, my boy got accepted into college."

Dawson: "Congrats bro!"

Thomas: "Thank you. Thank you. But um, you guys going to homecoming?"

Dawson: "Yea."

Casper: "Yea, imma' go."

Me: "N-n-n-nah, I-I-I-I'm not."

Casper: "Why? Don't tell me because of Deon now. Because you definitely ain't no threat to him."

Me: Nah, i-i-i-i-it a-a-a-a-ain't because of th-th-th-th-th-the that. I-I-I-I-I really don't c-c-c-care f-f-f-for it.

Thomas: Well, I know you're going to the pep rally at least because it's during school hours. Right?

Me: Y-y-y-yea, I-I-I-I-I-I guh-guh-guh-guh-guess I have n-n-n-no other option b-b-b-but to go.

(Female student walks over to our table with a box.)

Student: Hey gentleman, hope you all are having a great day. Don't forget to vote Jack Schuters and Ashley Wittmanton for homecoming king and queen. (Hands us paper slip with Ashley and Jack's name and the link to vote on our school website. Walks away.)

Dawson: "Ashley Who...?"

Me: "Remember, th-th-th-th-that wa-wa-wa-wa-one g-g-g-girl who you were l-l-l-l-l-looking at that I-I-I-I-I knew?"

Dawson: (Confused look)

Me: "On t-t-t-t-the f-f-f-first day?"

Dawson: "Oh. Ohhhh, her. Wait she goes out with Jack?"

Casper: "Which Jack?"

Dawson: "Jack Schuters."

Casper: "Oh, the one who wants to be black. Black Jack."

Thomas: "Yea, she talks about him all the time in class."

Dawson: "Man. He's lucky. So, who else is running for homecoming king and queen?"

Casper: "I know Deon and Freida are, but they'll probably win in the end though."

Thomas: "Aye, you know what? We should all be at the pep rally together."

Casper: "Yea that's cool."

Dawson: "Sounds good to me."

Me: "Ok."

Thomas: "Is anybody going to the game on Friday? It's supposed to be against one of the best teams."

Me: "Nah I-I-I-I-I'm not."

(Deon walks over to our table with Freida.)

Deon: "Aye fellas, how y'all feeling?"

Freida: (Waves.)

All except me: "We're feeling pretty good."

(Shakes everyone's hand except mine.)

Deon: "I just wanted to mention that me and my girl Freida are running for homecoming king and queen, and y'all should show us some love and vote for us. Alright, y'all have a good one now." (Walks away.)

Casper: "Marlin, you looked like you were about to try and hit him with a right uppercut bro."

Me: "That d-d-d-d-dude j-j-j-just gets on m-m-my nerves."

Thomas: But besides the fact, who are you guys going to vote for?

Dawson: Man, I would vote for Freida because of Deon, but Ashley is just too fine man. Shoot, I'll probably have to vote for her. I like Deon but Jack... I don't like him. He's too cocky. So, for me, it'll probably be Deon and Ashley.

Casper: Yea same. Ashley is cute. And Deon is cool.

Thomas: Well, you guys are bogus. I'll just vote for Deon and Freida. Sorry Marlin, I know you don't like him but like you said Dawson, Jack is super stuck up. And so is Deon, but at least he talks to other people outside of his group.

(Lunch comes to an end, students start to leave.)

Thomas: Alright guys, I'll see y'all on Friday for the pep rally.

Dawson, Casper, and I: Alright, see you bro (Shake hands and leave.)

After a few more of my classes ended, school finally came to an end. I got off at the bus stop and took an uber home so that I wouldn't have to walk alone in my neighborhood. Since I was off from work this day, I decided to dedicate this day to homework and practicing my speech. Julia was already home as her school wasn't far away from where we lived. I practiced my speech, repeatedly, trying not to stutter and remember the words.

Eventually, after practicing, I started to remember bits and pieces of my speech without having to look at the words on my paper, the words started to come to me almost naturally, and I thought, "Finally, I'm making progress." But I still couldn't get past the stuttering. Anytime that I would recite the words of the poem, there would be one part when I would get so caught up in my words or in my stutter where I couldn't even continue. It was like I couldn't talk after I got caught up in my stutter and lose my train of thought. But I just kept working at it. After I gave it a rest and started to work on my homework for my other classes, I practiced some more later that night then Mama came home from work.

Julia, who had just finished exercising, and I stopped what we were doing and came to the door to greet her as she continued to enter the house with no reaction. She closed the door and sat on the couch as she dropped her things down and stared at the ground. "What's wrong?" Julia asked. And after a long pause, Mama, with tears starting to fill her eyes finally replied, "Your Grandmother." "What about her?" We asked. Mama took a deep breath and said plainly, "She has lung cancer." Julia and I both responded with shock not knowing what to say.

"How? How she get it?" Julia asked. "I-I don't, I don't know. She doesn't know. It's just..." She paused and put her hands to her face and sobbed as tears began to roll from her eyes, sliding down her face and dropping from her jawline. We all just stood there, appalled. "Weh-weh-weh-well, we-we-where is she na-na-now?" I asked Mama. "She going back, in and out from the hospital. Here, go head give her a call. Check on her." Mama replied while digging into her purse and handing Julia and I, her phone. I took the phone and called her right there in front of Mama who was still in grief. Grandma picked up the phone. I put her on speaker phone, and we began to talk.

Grandma: (With a hoarse voice, sounding out of breath.) "Hello?"'

Julia: Hey Grandma, it's Julia. You feeling, ok?

Grandma: (After brief silence.) I-I-I'm doin' alright baby.

Me: Weh-Weh-Weh-Where ah-ah-ah-ah-are yu-yu-you n-n-now?

Grandma: I'm at hospital. They sayin' at the hospital that I got stage two lung cancer. They say I might need the surgery. And then they sayin' that it's a possibility that I could only have less than a year to live even if I get the surgery. We all gasped, looked at each other in surprise with our mouths wide open. Mama starts tearing up even more. But let me tell y'all something, I know God ain't bring me this far to leave me. And I know He is able to do exceedingly abundantly above all I could ask or think. According to His power. It's His will that will be done in my life, and I know that it's His will that I prosper and be in health as He said in His word. It's not my time to go yet. I know that for a fact. And can't no doctor, no devil, or no person tell me that it is.

Mama, Julia, and I: (Prolonged silence.)

Grandma: "Y'all awfully quite over there. What, y'all don't believe? Where's y'all faith? I keep tryna' tell y'all that there's value beyond the visual. Whatever that visual may be, whether it's sickness, poverty, lack, your environment, or even how you look, there's a greater value behind it. Anything that you see that's going on around you or what you see when you get up to look in the mirror in the morning is a visual. And behind that visual there's value, and the value behind that visual is waiting to manifest. Waiting to be released. But only if we acknowledge it, believe in it, and let God bring it out of us by having faith in Him and if we humble ourselves to Him."

Mama: (Whispering.) "Let me know when y'all finished" (Gets up and walks away.)

Julia: (Starting to cry.) "But why, why Grandma? Why God let you have cancer and then only let you have a year left to live?"

Grandma: "Baby, everything that you to go through isn't always a punishment. Not everything. Some things that happen is a consequence of the things that you've done, but what God lets you go through can be used to make your faith in Him stronger. Because when things get rough, it forces you to call on Him, to lean upon Him even more so than before. (Coughs.) And baby when you call on Him, truthfully and sincerely, He will answer and come nigh. (Meaning near.) And when that happens, it makes your belief, trust, and faith in Him stronger. Because when He's nigh, He changes you and your situation. And that's the value in my visual. To be made stronger in all areas in my walk with Him because I know He is making me stronger. This sickness is not unto death, but for His glory like He said. So y'all don't worry about me because God got me. And He got y'all too! Pray for me now. But everything's going to be ok. And Marlin, you get ready. Because God is about to do something amazing in your life. You just wait and see."

Me: "Y-y-y-y-yes, m-m-m-m-m-m-ma'am."

Grandma: "Alright now babies your grandma is a little tired so I'll have to talk to y'all later now. But remember what I said, everything you go through isn't always a punishment or consequence of what you done. But it's what the Lord uses to make us stronger. Now in what way that it makes each individual person better and stronger is different, but I know that He works all things for the good of those who love Him. Alright? Ok, bye-bye now."

Julia and I: "Bye Grandma."

"Man." I thought to myself. This one really hit hard. If it wasn't already bad enough for me that we were struggling financially, that I didn't have a real way of transportation besides taking the bus, and that I didn't know how I was going to even get into college. It was already bad enough that my grades were low, that I had to work for idiots with idiots, and that I was an outcast at school not being able to fit in. It was bad enough that I was surrounded by gang violence at home and surrounded by pressure to fall into drug use. But now this. The one person in my life besides my sister and Mama who could empower, inspire, motivate, and encourage me to be somebody, was being taken from me. Why? Even though Grandma was very optimistic about what she was going through, I knew that it was a chance that she could still die as cancer is said to be one of the leading causes of deaths in adults who are in their late forties, fifties, and early sixties.

I thought to myself that if she died what would help us keep this family strong? Who would be the person I would turn to if I needed advice or uplifting? Mama was always working, so Grandma was really the only person I could turn to. But now there was a likelihood that she could be gone.

Julia looked up at me, asking, "Now what we gone do?" I responded by shrugging my shoulders as Julia curled up on the couch. I walked towards the back of the house to see where Mama went. As I went past the bathroom, I saw her staring at herself in the mirror. "Ma?" I asked her. I walked in and gave her a hug. I wasn't sure why she was looking at herself the way that she was. She wasn't saying anything but still hugged me back. I began to assume that it was something that she wanted to tell me but didn't.

Like I said, there was never an explanation for the awkward relationship between her and Grandma, but now I was really starting to get curious. Why did Mama just get up and walk away in the middle of Grandma talking? It had to have been something that Grandma was saying that Mama didn't want to hear, but I couldn't put my finger on it. Usually, when people would get up and walk away from situations like this to end up like the way Mama was now, it told me that they either felt guilty about something or that they didn't want a part of them to be exposed.

Mama wiped her face to clear it from her tears and went into the kitchen to go cook a quick meal for the morning. Initially, I thought that I would have stayed up for a little while longer to practice my speech, but after this news, I no longer had a drive to do it. I felt demotivated, crushed on the inside. But I started to think on the words that Grandma said to us. The one that stood out to me was when she said that the things that we go through are not always punishment, but rather a way for God to make us stronger by causing us to call on Him, humbling ourselves. I remember saying to myself that everything that I was experiencing felt like punishment. And it made sense because I didn't feel as if I did anything that wrong to where I had to go through what I was going through and cause me to be in the position that I was in. Maybe God really was trying to get through to me. Maybe God really was trying to help me be stronger, better, in whatever areas that I needed to be.

And on top of that, Grandma did tell me to get ready because something big was about to happen for me. Knowing my grandma, it was like whatever she predicted for the future usually ended up happening. Maybe the big change that she said would happen for me was me getting good grades this year, something that never happened before. It would have to start with me doing well on my speech this Friday and getting a good grade on it. Although I knew that I stuttered badly, I still believed God would take away that stutter and allow me to speak clearly so that I could do well and overcome.

This had to be it. This year had to be the time where I would receive all the answers to the prayers that I prayed. This had to be the time where all the work I put in over the years gets paid off. I was certain that it was all going to start this Friday with my speech. I felt that with this new feeling of hope and desire that came from what Grandma said was going to happen, I could present the best speech I ever gave in my life. Even possibly the best speech presented in the class. Stutter free, clearly spoken, and fluent. With this thought process, it re-motivated me to practice on my speech. I practiced, prayed for a little bit, and went to sleep.

Chapter 7: The Breaking Point

It was a Thursday afternoon, and it was the last class before school was out. Usually, when it was the last class, there would be a hyped feeling in the air as all the students were ready to go home and get into their after-school routines. But today, I had to work after school. There was about fifteen minutes of class left, and I was just finishing up an in-class assignment that was to be turned in by the end of class. And sooner than I knew it, I finished and awaited the sound of the bell so I could go about the rest of my day.

Then finally, the bell rung at 3pm, and it was time for me to start getting ready for work. I had to be at work at 4pm. In my spare time I decided to go to the lobby again. As I was walking outside towards the lobby, I saw Deon in the parking lot half dressed for football practice in an athletic t-shirt and shorts standing next to Freida and Ashley as they were talking next to his car. I saw Deon turn his head looking in my direction and stare at me as Ashley and Freida did the same. I couldn't hear what they were saying, but I saw that they were laughing alternating between turning their heads towards me and then to each other. And I knew immediately that they were making jokes about me. I heard Ashley suddenly just outburst in laugher stepping away from the group while cracking up at me, evidently, as I continued to walk past. I saw her make her way back towards Deon and Freida and heard her say to them, "OH MY GOD, Y'ALL FUNNY! BUT Y'ALL RIGHT THOUGH, HE DO BE LOOKIN' UGLY!", as she continued to laugh with them.

Being where I was from, the old me would have gone over to Deon since we were out of school and did something wild like fight him in a crazy, reckless way. But since I was older now, I didn't want to do anything that would distract me from my goal or that would cause God to make me reap a bad harvest for bad seeds being sown or what some would call karma. I continued to walk past, ignoring it as I felt that this would be the Christian thing to do.

And even though I still felt unsure whether God saw me as one of His children, or if I was good enough for Him to consider me a Christian, I didn't want to do anything that would make Him disappointed in me. I admit that I had my questions about God. I admit that I didn't understand why He let certain things happen and didn't let other things happen. I admit that I felt like He didn't answer my prayers and felt like

He was ignoring me at times. I admit that I doubted Him from time to time. I admit that I often felt like I was being punished by Him for no apparent reason which led me to waver in my faith in Him.

But through all of this I wanted to still be perfect in His eyes and maintain that love I had for God. Even though He may have been a figment of other's imaginations, He was real to me, although I've never seen Him before. Recently, I've been having this feeling like fire on the inside of me. This feeling like I was excited about something positive and this feeling of something building up in me. I had no clue what it was, but I knew it had to be something related to God.

Lately, I've been thinking about Jesus, His sacrifice, and His love that He is said to have a lot more than usual. I knew that He loved me. I heard it all before, but I didn't feel like it because of my current situation. But like Grandma said, maybe all this turmoil, stress, and anxiety wasn't God punishing me but Him training me to make me stronger.

I went into the lobby and sat down. I pulled out my speech and practice it for tomorrow morning as a few students walked past. After about ten minutes, I saw Dawson and Casper approach me and greet me with our handshake.

129

Dawson: "Yo Marlin, what you doing over here? I hope you're not over here daydreaming about my girl Ashley."

Casper: "But bro, did you see her in her practice cheergear?"

Dawson: "Oh, yea bro! She is so fine, I can't lie." (Smiling.)

Me: (Chuckling.)

Dawson: "But anyways what are you doing over here Marlin?"

Me: "I-I-I-I-I-I'm w-wu-wu-waiting for m-m-m-my work shift to s-s-s-s-start."

Dawson: "Oh, ok."

Casper: (Checks phone.) "Look bro, they just posted again." (Shows phone to Dawson.)

(Hip-hop music starts playing.)

Dawson: "AYE!!" (Starts moving to music playing while watching the phone.)

Me: "Hu-Hu-Hu-Hu-Hu-Who that?"

Casper: (Shows me his phone.)

(It was Jahmoni and his dancing clique that I encountered a while back.)

Me: "Oh, I-I-I-I-I-I na-na-know them."

Dawson and Casper: (Looking confused.) '

Dawson: "Like know them personally, or just know about them?"

Me: "I-I-I-I-I know th-th-th-th-them p-p-p-personally. They f-f-f-f-f-from m-m-my hood. And n-n-n-not to l-l-l-long ago, they a-a-a-a-asked me i-i-i-i-if I wanted t-t-to join they lil' clique too."

Casper: "Bro, that's so cool. You should do it; I mean they're about blow."

Dawson: "But Marlin you're terrible at dancing, and you're not a musical guy either. No offense, I'm just saying."

Me: "Th-th-th-they w-w-w-w-wanted me to b-b-b-b-be like th-they camera guy or s-s-s-something."

Casper: "Nah, but seriously, you should consider that though. I mean these boys are really talented. And if you join them and they get famous, then you're on your way too with them. Like bro, there's no telling what can happen. I think you should give it a try."

Dawson: "Yea, Casper is right though, if you join their group you'll get on their level and it could help you start your own videography career or something, in addition to getting paid from th…Wait, are they going to pay you for filming them?"

Me: "Th-th-th-th-that's wh-whu-whu-what they said."

Dawson: "Dude…"

Casper: "Bro that's a huge opportunity. I would take it to be honest. But anyways bro, we're going to head out because we got to make up a test. But I'll see you tomorrow at pep rally, right?"

Me: "Alright."

Dawson: "And get Ashley off your mind too, because you know you ain't gonna get with that." (Laughing with Casper)

That was interesting. It was now apparent to me that Jahmoni and his little dancing clique that he had formed were more popular than what I had thought. But I still wasn't sold out on joining their clique because I still felt that my new goal and route would provide a more stable and secure future for me. But I can say that they were who they said they were and did exactly what they said they did which I respected.

As I continued with my studying, I looked up and saw our school advertising our homecoming game on the TV. The scene cut to the football field during their practice to interview some of our key players. After the first few people, they interviewed Deon. The interviewer asked if he did anything special to prepare for the game and Deon responded by saying that he didn't want to give "too much information" after smiling but said that he had trained, practiced hard, and maintained his focus. Then, the camera switched to interviewing cheerleaders as Ashley appeared on the screen. The interviewer asked Ashley what was the most exciting about cheering for the football team.

"The most exciting thing about cheering for the football team is seeing how everyone becomes one and becomes a family when they see our team play. Even though I just transferred here, I can feel the positive energy. I think it's a really special thing, and whoever does not enjoy it just must not like to be entertained or not know how to have fun." Ashley said.

Seeing this just irritated me all over again and it had nothing to do with me being jealous of their status, notoriety, or platform. It was the fact that they could basically do whatever they wanted and talk about me, a good kid at heart, whenever they felt like it and still got praise from everyone in school. Why? Because they were popular, gifted, intelligent, and had nearly everyone in school as their supporters. While I was the opposite. With all the things that God blessed them with, they chose to be cocky about it but get rewarded while I suffered in silence. As I remember Mama always telling me, that everyone who exalted themselves shall be humbled, it seemed as if there was an exception for these two. It was obvious to me how arrogant Deon and Ashley were, as they constantly put themselves above me and over me with their actions and words.

As I mentioned before, I truly loved God, but I didn't understand why He would let some things happen for some but not others. This very situation with Deon and Ashley was one of them. It was like they could do whatever they wanted and in return got everything that they needed and wanted despite me trying my best to serve God and had next to nothing. For the record, I couldn't even enjoy watching my school football team play anymore despite them being a good team because of how the star players were. They thought that they were all that and better than everybody else and let the other people who were "below" them know about it.

I honestly just wanted this year to be over. But at the same time, I wasn't because I still didn't even know what I was going to do, where I was going to go, or how I was going to do after high school. Yea, I may have had this new goal, but I wasn't that confident in myself. My new goal for my life was just becoming more of a wish more so than a plan the more I thought about it. So here I am, stuck in the middle of a rock and a hard place. I was going through a hard time, that felt like it would never end. Realistically, I had nothing to look forward to unless some miracle happened which probably wasn't going to happen. But at least, I knew that tomorrow could be a start to something fresh and could possibly be a chance to get me on the right path if I did well on my speech.

I looked on my phone and it was time for me to start heading to work. I got to work and after my first hour there it was already turning out to be a disaster. The main manager Mike wasn't there but the assistant managers were and kept accusing me of being slothful while pushing me to "work harder". Now to be fair, I was moving a little slow, but I was tired from all the things that happened this week. From Grandma being sick, to my upcoming speech, in addition to the buildup of my anxious thoughts about the possibility of me not doing well this year resulting in me not having anywhere to go.

But I wasn't moving slow enough to where I felt that they needed to continually call me out on it.

Of course, Bruno had to be there. Even though he wasn't snitching on me as he would usually do, it was clear to me that he tried to one up me on everything that I did to make himself appear to the managers that he was better than me. But honestly, I didn't care to compete with him. Throughout my whole shift I had to deal with the assistant manager telling me how Bruno was out working me and doing a better job even though Bruno was only "working hard" because it was his duty to outshine me. It wasn't as busy of a day, so my body didn't feel as tired from work, but I was still ready to go home.

I got my stuff together to leave and one of the assistant managers approached me and asked if he could talk to me in private in the back office. He sat down in his chair and pointed me to a seat. "Marlin." He said as he pulled out a folder looking for a specific sheet leaning in towards me. "You were never a bad worker at least as I see it. But the thing is, we're getting an overflow of workers who are starting to come in and it turns out that our sales revenue has been lower than usual. So, the bad news is, we'll have to cut your hours. But on the bright side you can keep your job, we won't lay you off." I sat there with no expression on my face. Typically, I worked three to four days a week which totaled around twelve to fifteen hours per week. "But uh, you're in school anyways, right?" The assistant manager asked. I shook my head yes. "Alright then, that should give you some time to focus more on your schoolwork." The manager said. I asked him how many days that I would work each week.

"Well…" The manager said while scratching his head. "Ideally, I'd like to get you to have three days but for now it looks like we'll have to just stick with one day a week after this Saturday. Preferably on Saturday's so you could at least have a longer shift. I'm sorry but that's the best I could do. Is that alright?" I took a deep breath in, sighed, and responded by shaking my head yes. He then dismissed me from his office, and I went on my way. Grandma would have a uber waiting for me now on the days that I worked, now that "Auntie" went missing in action.

Throughout the car ride, I thought about how my hours were being cut to work up to only one shift per week. I realized that the money that I would make from working one day each week wouldn't be enough to help Mama in our situation. I thought of how much of the money that I made in the past since I started working at fourteen went to Mama to help her pay the bills. But now, since I only had to work one day each week on a minimum hourly wage, I would barely be able to sustain my family or myself. Here I am scared, anxious, and irritated all over again. How would I be able to support Mama now?

The thought of seeing Mama and Julia struggle and go through even harder times rattled me. It shook me to my core knowing that at any moment, Mama could miss a couple payments and get so behind on the bills that we could go without something that we needed to live or even get evicted. Or that any moment, they could be robbed and even shot over the little things that we had. I felt a sense of panic, nervousness, and fear. What was I going to do now? How was I going to provide for my family? It was like everything was going downhill.

The only thing I had left to give me any positivity was the speech I had to present tomorrow and that was if I did well on it. With all these situations happening all at once, I already felt so drained to where I had a feeling that I wasn't going to do well. I got into the house after the uber driver, at one point, drove us through a bunch of people that appeared to be in a gang flashing their gang signs at us while staring into the car and had their guns visibly showing through their pants.

I finally made it home sitting at the kitchen table and Mama came in shortly after me. "Whew, Lord have mercy!! My goodness, them boys is sho' nuff out there." She said while entering the house closing and locking the front door. "POP! PA-POP! POP! POP!" "Lord Jesus. Here they go again. JULIA, GET AWAY FROM THAT WINDOW! THEY SHOOTIN'!" I heard Mama shout to Julia as she walked further into the house.

When Mama came in, we began to talk about how work and school went. I didn't want to tell her that my hours were cut because I didn't want her to panic or get nervous. Instead, I reminded her of the speech tomorrow. After that, she went to the back towards Julia's room to see if she was ok. "Julia?" Mama asked in concern while turning on the light. "Yes?" Julia responded being curled under the covers avoiding the window. Mama and I squatted down below the window level as the sound of sirens passed down our block.

I saw the worry in Julia's eyes, fearing the possibility of a bullet penetrating through the window into her room, as Mama put her hand on her hip that was sticking out from the blanket. Mama looked down at the ground, staring at it for a while rubbing Julia's leg. Then she finally proceeded to say, "Y'all know this was never my intentions, right? I never wanted us as a family to go through this. But y'all daddies ain't know no better so… we're here now. It's not much we can do about it. I try to be there for y'all, and I appreciate every moment of time spent with y'all." I heard Mama's voice crack as she started to tear up and get emotional. "And I don't know what God is doing, but we gotta' trust Him. Like I tell y'all again and again, be humble, stay humble, because whoever humbles themselves will be exalted, and whoever exalts themselves will be humbled." Mama added as she brought us together for a hug.

Afterwards, Mama and I walked out of Julia's room, and I told her that I was going to bed so I could be ready in the morning. I gave her hug before I went to bed and headed towards my room to put on my night clothes. Before I got to my room, I heard Mama say, "Marlin… Son, Mama is proud of you." I turned around and told her thank you and that I was proud of her too. I was so anxious about tomorrow that when I got in my bed, it was hard for me to fall asleep. I kept thinking about the possibility of me messing up and stuttering in front of everyone. I knew my speech well, not necessarily word for word, but I felt that I knew it well enough for me to recite it properly and pass with a decent grade. It was my delivery that I was concerned about, so I hoped for the best.

As I continued to think, sleep started to fall upon me rather quickly. With all the things going on in my life right now, from Grandma getting sick, working hard just to get my hours cut at work, and the stress of delivering a major speech in front an audience that already misunderstood me as a person, I was tired. So tired that my tiredness outweighed my anxiousness. Before I knew it, I was fast asleep, totally unconscious of the outside noises of the streets.

I woke up the next morning and instantly marked it as a special day in my mind. This day, I believed, was the day that would be the start of something big that God would do just as Grandma said. Why wouldn't it be? This was the perfect opportunity for God to turn my situation around. This was the day that the Lord had made, so I decided to be glad and rejoice in it. With this mindset for this day, it didn't matter what someone else said, how someone else felt, or what they did because I got my hopes up very high and believed.

I did my usual morning routine and arrived at school. I tried practicing memorizing bits and pieces of my speech on my way to school by reciting them to myself, but each time I would either get the lines mixed up, forget some words, or lose my train of thought. Because of this it made me feel uneasy and a little bit unconfident in myself. I started to doubt myself, and the closer time got for class, the more nervous, anxious, and reluctant I felt about my speech. After seeing how my practice went this morning, it didn't look like I was going to do well on this speech. Considering how badly I stuttered in addition to Deon and Ashley being there watching me made it even worse. But at this point all I could do is hope and believe for the best. And that's exactly what I did.

I only had a few minutes before class started, so I went to a quiet area to get my last practice. The closer I got to class; the more reality started to sink in. With all the work that I put in, this moment could be the time where the trajectory of my life changed. Why wouldn't it be? I mean, I felt God loved me enough to at least let me do well on this speech to boost my grade.

Not to say that I expected this speech to be a determinant of where I would end up in life, but I knew that if everything went as planned, it would set me on the track that I needed to accomplish my goal for this year and move forward. I desperately needed a boost in my grade, help with my GPA, and acceptance into college to accomplish my overall goal of getting out of the hood. I tried not to tie this one speech to my success for this year, but it was hard not to. The teacher already mentioned how he would grade us strictly and that this speech was a large portion of our grade.

I walked through the class door, as everyone who was in the class was practicing for their speeches. "Alrighty, you guys know what today is. Hope you all are ready and have been practicing." Mr. Wysol said as he got up from his desk. Instantly the anxiousness, nervousness, and worry doubled. I couldn't control it and I couldn't stop it. I looked around the class to see how the other students looked as they appeared more prepared than nervous.

"Let's not waste any time and get started right away, shall we? But before I start calling out any names, do I have any volunteers?" He asked. The room went silent as everybody hesitated and avoided making eye-contact with him. I looked around the room, hoping that someone would volunteer themselves so that I wouldn't have to worry about being called on first. The room continued to stay silent, until I finally heard someone say, "Me! So, I can get this over with." I looked over and saw Ashley raise her hand while getting up. "Oh, great! That was a close call!" Mr. Wysol said before relaying classroom procedures. "Now remember class, we are all going to remain respectful to each student who performs their speech. That means no laughing or talking while they speak. We will all give them our undivided attention and clap when they are finished. Let's all show respect." He finally added before he demanded that we pay attention to Ashley as she stood in front of the class.

Since our speech had to be memorized, we weren't allowed to use paper or notecard to help us. It had to be pure memorization. So there Ashley stood, empty handed glancing at the teacher as he gave her the nod to start her speech presentation. Ashley took a deep breath and began to recite her poetic speech fluently almost with ease. She seemed so comfortable while doing so. She didn't stutter, take long pauses, and spoke loudly and clear the entire time. She barely had any mistakes and seemed as if she was programmed to remember the entire speech.

After she finished, everybody clapped for her, and she returned to her seat. The teacher remained in his seat writing a few things down in the silence of the classroom. "Alright, who's next?!" He asked shouting out loud. "I'll go!" Deon shouted as he got up from his spot and went up to the front. "Alright, we got the superstar up next!" Mr. Wysol said with excitement. Deon made his way up to the front and immediately after the teacher gave him the go ahead to start his speech, Deon started to recite his poetic speech word for word, line for line, without any hesitation, pauses, or breaks. He finished right on the dot within the required time. "Wow!" Mr. Wysol responded, as everybody clapped passionately. Mr. Wysol continued writing down the results of Deon's performance.

"Alright, next?" He asked as everybody remained quiet, sitting in the dead silence that filled the room. "Anybody?" He continued in his petition. Still, everybody remained silent. "So, it looks like I'll have to refer to the list." He said as he started flipping through a notebook. He then called out a name of a student in the class, leaving the student with no choice but to present his speech. He went to the list again and call out a second student.

There was silence again as no one volunteered and showed passive behavior. Everyone who had presented their speech up until this point did well. Usually during a day of speeches, the first couple of presenters set the standard for that day. Meaning that if the first few performers did well, then the rest of the class would expect the following presenter to do just as good. And if one presenter did worse than all the other presenters, it would make their bad performance more memorable. But by the way things were looking, it could be a possibility that I wouldn't have to present my speech today.

Four people presented and only about five or six people would be able to present today because of our shortened class periods for the pep rally. Even though I practiced to the point where most people would have been prepared, I lacked the confidence. I felt that if I had some extra time, it would give me the confidence I needed to do well. I hoped that my name wouldn't be called today.

Mr. Wysol finished up the last of his writing, got up and looked on the list and called out a name. The first time, no response. The second time, still no response and he then came to realize that the person who he was calling was absent. He then decided to skip to the next person on the list saying, "Uh, the next person on the list is…Marlin! Marlin, you're up!"

At that very moment, it felt like something hit me. My heart sank to bottom of my chest. My stomach turned inside out. My breath was shortened, and my veins turned into a racetrack because of the blood racing inside of me. The only thing I could associate with this feeling was panic, nervousness and anxiety about performing my speech. There was nothing I could do, think, or say to get rid of it in this moment. I got up from my seat in terror knowing that I had to present an entire poetic speech, that I didn't even completely remember, in front of a whole class that included those who preyed on me and witnessed my constant downfall.

As I started to walk up to the front of the class, all the students looked at me strangely because they knew that I was different. It was like they sensed it and I could perceive that they knew that I came from a lower quality of living than them by the way they were looking at me. I walked up to the front feeling as if I transitioned into an alternative reality with every step that I took. Finally, I got up to the front of the class and stood there as everyone stared at me waiting for me to say something. The feeling was so surreal. I stood there for a while before hearing Mr. Wysol say, "Alright Marlin, it's yours."

I nervously surveyed the class before I spoke and opened my mouth to recite my poetic speech. I started to recite the speech that I somewhat memorized.

Me: "Did you know, the tr.... The tr-tr-tr-tr-tr-tr-tr... Th-th-th-th-the the t-tr-tr-tr-tr-tr-tr-t-tr... (Stopping and starting over.) D-d-d-did you know the tr-tr-tr-tr-tr... Tr-tr-tr-tr-t-tr..."

"OH MY GOSH!" I thought to myself. I couldn't even get the first sentence out. As I struggled to get through the first sentence, I watched the reactions on everyone's faces. Some were surprised at how much I stuttered. Some looked like they were experiencing secondhand embarrassment from me, and others looked like they were ready to burst in laughter. Ashley put her head down as if she was on her phone as I saw Deon looking at me with a smirk on his face. I never saw a speech pathologist when I attended elementary and junior high school back home because most schools in my neighborhood didn't offer them. It wasn't until my freshmen year that I started seeing a speech pathologist.

Usually, they would tell me that if I ever got into a deep stutter, that it would be best for me to stop talking altogether and restart with my sentence. But in this case, it didn't seem to work, but I'd figure I would give it a few more tries. I went on ahead again, continuing with my speech.

Me: (Stopping and restarting my speech, taking a deep breath.) Did you know, th-th-th-the tr-tr-trouble of making wa-wa-wa-wa-wa-wa-one… One, uh, wa-wa-wa-wa-wa-one…Wa-wa-one um…One…Wa-wa-one…Um…Uhh…"

At this point I was so rattled that my mind was all over the place. I couldn't even remember the rest of my speech after this part. Knowing that I still had minutes left on the time clock, that the whole class was watching me in secondhand embarrassment, and that people were going to make fun of me afterwards, I panicked. Panicking caused my mind to black out. I promise it was much smoother when I was practicing at home. I was panicking and hyperventilating. I was shook and insecure and felt as if I couldn't talk or remember my speech for the life of me. I just wanted it to be over. I tried to speak again, and the words wouldn't come out right.

I concluded that it would be best for me to go sit down and be done with it. After remaining silent while staring at the ground for a while, I decided that's what I would do. I looked at the teacher who looked concerned for me and went and sat back down.

Everybody had a surprised look on their face and tried their best not to look at me. I heard one person clap as more people started to clap. After everyone clapped for my terrible presentation, Mr. Wysol proceeded to say, "Well... Uh, we only have a few minutes left and I don't think we'll have enough time for another speech to be completed, so we'll continue speeches on Monday. So, you all can just talk amongst yourselves for the time being. Thank you to my presenters who presented today, and I have your presentations graded so I'll hand them out now."

He handed me mine face down on my desk while squatting down requesting to see me after class. I didn't want to even see what grade I got as I already knew that it was going to be a 'F'. But I hoped that somehow, at least a 'C' would appear on the other side of the paper. But I had to see it for myself. So, I flipped over the piece of paper to the other side and saw that I received a 'F'. I looked around as Deon, Ashley, and other students in the class were talking about their speech.

Other students in class grouped around them to join in saying, "Y'all did good!" Again, seemingly out of nowhere, their heads one by one, turned towards me. I saw some looking at me laughing while the others stared plainly. I heard Deon speaking to the group quietly, thinking that I wouldn't hear him. Right as they were staring the bell rung and everybody got up to go to their next class. The teacher dismissed us but insisted that I stay. In embarrassment, anger, and frustration, I walked out of the class with all the other students ignoring Mr. Wysol who was yelling my name.

I went straight to my next class so that I didn't have to face the criticisms of the class. But again, why? Why me? I didn't even feel like going into a whole mental rant again about why God was allowing these horrible things to continue to happen to me. But this was my last chance at bringing a positive outcome out of my life. And I FAILED! Not only did I fail, but I failed with God supposedly "on my side." But if He was on my side, how could I have failed?

At this point I knew and was fully convinced that God wasn't on my side. Matter of fact, I doubted whether He was on my side to begin with. He probably didn't even care that much about me. For all I know, I could have been created to be God's laughingstock. Maybe that's why He created me, maybe that was my purpose. So that He could be entertained by everything that was taking place in my life. So much for my life. What life? At this point I wanted to consider myself done with God. Done with this Christian walk. Who cares about what my grandma said? it didn't look like anything that she said would happen was going to happen.

Lunchtime rolled around, and I made my way to the cafeteria. Since today was the day of the pep rally, we could go right from lunch to the field for the pep rally. So, I decided not to eat since I lost my appetite because of how poorly I did on my speech. My spirit was down. So, I went to the table where Thomas and his friends were sitting as always.

Thomas: Aye wassup Marlin?

Me: (Silence.)

Thomas: Wassup?

Me: (Silence.)

Thomas: Ok then. Wassup with you guys?

Casper: Oh, I'm good bro! I'm talking to this new girl, and she is fine like look... (Pulls out phone to show picture.) Look!

Dawson: Eh, she ok.

Thomas: I mean she's not bad looking.

Casper: Man, y'all just hating on me. But anyway, y'all ready for that pep rally?

Thomas: Yea. And like I said we all got stick together so we can sit together.

Dawson: Yea that's a plan. So, Marlin, how'd that speech go?

Me: (Silence.)

Dawson: Huh?

Me: (Silence.)

Dawson: Hello, I'm talking to your lil...

Me: BOY SH-SH-SH-SHUT UP!!!! Y-Y-YOU TALK TO M-M-M-MUCH!!! (Slamming on the lunch table, drawing attention from everyone nearby, and causing a scene.)

Everyone at table: (Silence. Security guard walks over.)

Security Guard: Is everything alright over here?

Thomas: Yeah, they weren't serious they were just playing.

Security Guard: Well, it didn't look like it but make sure you guys keep your hands to yourselves. If not, then we won't. Ok? (Walks Away.)

Thomas: Uh, well... Um, but we're all still going to the pep rally together, right?

Casper and Dawson: Yea.

I didn't feel like talking and I wasn't going to talk. I let them continue to talk amongst themselves as I remained quiet and stayed to myself while they just left me alone. They looked at me occasionally and appeared to be fearful of me possible doing something to them. Although I was considered to be soft amongst most people back in my hood, it was another thing when I got angry.

As they talked without me saying a word, lunchtime finally came to an end. They got up together as I got up and started walking the opposite way. I didn't care how they would respond, and I didn't care what they thought. I went my separate path making my way to the field. I couldn't just walk off campus from this school as opposed to the unsupervised and disorderly schools back home.

I went and got on the pathway to the field by myself: lonely, frustrated, annoyed, mad, sad, and everything else. While everybody else was cheering and excited, turning up with their friends, here I am alone. Feeling nothing but negativity.

I got to the field where I could feel the vibrations of the percussion instruments inside of my body. The mascots clowned around and paraded themselves while everybody screamed and yelled. I walked up to the bleachers and sat in the senior section as everybody in their groups of friends started to crowd me.

Like most pep rallies, our pep rally included the routines done by cheerleaders at our games. So, the cheerleaders, pom girls, and the male athletes who were on the football and basketball teams came out. The cheerleaders started their routine as the intro to a recent hit rap song started to play which was followed with a beat drop that blasted through the speakers.

As they began their routine, I saw Ashley front in center. Then, everybody formulated in what was like a half circle. There stood Ashley in the middle. She took a few steps back, then ran and jumped into a cartwheel, which turned into a double back flip, launching herself in the air, doing a mid-air twist and then landed almost perfectly on her feet. Everybody shouted after she landed on her feet and cheered. Then Freida came out next doing another stunning flip that left everybody in awe.

After a few more events involving our school football team and students going against faculty members, the pep rally started to whine down. The announcers called all the homecoming king and queen candidates to come forth. They went through each candidate individually, calling out their names as people cheered, an indication of who would win. Amongst the people who got the most cheers, were Deon and Ashley. Not Freida or Jack even though they were the ones who were Deon and Ashley's significant others which was strange, but at this point I could care less.

After the pep rally ended and all the announcements were made about the homecoming game and dance, we were dismissed from the pep rally and free to go home. But as for me, I had to work. So as always, I went to the lobby to wait for my shift to start. As I sat down, I began to think.

My goal, my dream, my plan that I had to live a better life was now pretty much non-existent. My only hope to bring into manifestation had now been diminished. I knew for a fact that I had a 'F' in my English class right now. As Mr. Wysol said, if we did poorly on this, it would be hard to come back from. This class was mandatory for me to graduate, which meant that if I didn't pass this class, I wouldn't be able to graduate high school and attend college. With everything going on in my life right now, I was too tired to try and do anything else to bring my grade up.

So much for being a therapist, so much for going to college, and so much for all the work, praying, and believing I did to try and help me get to that place. It was over for me. I had no clue what I could do next. It was obvious that I wasn't going anywhere with school, and I couldn't use music, athletics, or arts to try and make a way for myself. To make matters even worse, I didn't have any real job, business, or person to fall back on. I got my hours cut working for these goofies who didn't even care about me. I had nothing legal that I could sell to make a side income from. Mama was still struggling with making ends meet, and Grandma was sick so she was starting to accumulate hospital bills in addition to her not being available as much as she used to be so that I could talk with her.

I had nothing to look forward to, yet I still had to suffer through all the pain I was going through. Out of nowhere, for the first time, a random thought within me arose and I started to consider it. Suicide. Wait no! NO, NO, NO, NO! I couldn't do that. I'm stronger than that I thought to myself. So, I immediately tried to exile that thought out of my head.

But then as I did that, another thought popped up. The thought of me being like my father and trying to sell drugs to make a living, dropping out of school. Then another thought popped up, a vision, of me robbing someone with a gun. With all these thoughts starting to circulate I shouted out in frustration, "AAAAHH!!" The people who were passing nearby from the pep rally looked at me in confusion as if I was some kind of wild animal.

It was now getting real for me. The cares and issues of life were beating me down, and there was no way for me to escape. So, I just sat there. As the thoughts kept coming and circling around in my head. Drugs, suicide, depression, robbery, gangbanging, and evil things. The thing was, I knew these thoughts weren't even my typical thoughts. Of course, in my neighborhood, I was surrounded by these things on a daily. But I always tried to envision myself doing something greater, above these things. Until now. Because I felt that there was nothing else for me to do, no other options, and that despite how hard I tried, there was nothing that would ever work.

I thought about dropping out of school, to pursue another life on a whim. But I remembered that if I ever tried that, Mama would probably kick me out. But I knew that if I didn't find another alternative soon, I would eventually get too old to live at home with Ma without making any contribution to the family. I started thinking about me being in my thirties still living with Mama, and that was if I even made it to that age. I didn't know what I was going to do in the long-run or for the moment. But anyways, it was time for me to go to work so I got up and headed towards the exit of the lobby.

As I passed by the hallway, I saw Deon alone with Ashley, as they were all close together in each other's faces looking as if they were about to kiss against the wall. I looked for a split second and continued to head out as I heard them laughing together when I left out the door.

I dismissed what I saw because I knew if I told anyone it would be a problem. I got to work and did my job as usual. But this time I was so ready to snap. Thankfully Bruno wasn't there but Mike was, and he kept looking at me to see if I was doing my job. Although he didn't say anything to me, this just made me mad. But sooner than later, my shift was over, and it was time for me to go home.

As I was leaving, Mike called me. I looked over my shoulder and he waved me over. So, I hesitantly came over because I was already angry about the day. When I got within reasonable distance of him, he pointed to a small trash can that was still a third full. I looked at him, he looked at me. "So, you're really gonna' just stand there? Take it out! This should've been done at least an hour ago." He said. But still I continued to just stare at him wanting to hit him in the face. At this point, I quite frankly didn't care about anything in life anymore. To avoid any extra conflict, I did it even though I had already clocked out.

The uber pulled up and I got in. On the way home, I watched the uber driver shake as he passed through my neighborhood looking scared. I got out without saying thank you or anything because at this point, I was too far from the real Marlin. I lost my dreams, passion, aspirations, hope, and vision. I walked in the house and went straight to bed.

With everything going on, I felt my heart getting colder. I was tired of being broke. Tired of barely passing school. Tired of worrying about the future, and if I would end up dead, in jail, or in the streets. Tired of being laughed at. Tired of trying yet seeing no result. Tired of watching my family struggle. Tired of the environment that I was in.

I was tired of being ignored by God and trying to serve him. I was getting tired of always trying to do the right thing. Tired of trying to live the "Christian" life yet struggling in almost every area of life just to see myself in this position.

So, I made my mind up that I didn't care anymore about anything. Why should I? It's not that I wanted to be rebellious and be running the streets. But what else was there for me to do especially since God didn't provide this opportunity for today? If I gangbanged, I gangbanged. So what? If I sold drugs, I sold drugs. What difference would it make?

Despite the thoughts that I was thinking, deep down inside, I knew that all I really wanted was for my family and I to be out of this environment, to be in my right mind at peace within myself, making a positive impact on others, all while being right with God. But at this point, I was convinced that He wasn't at all concerned about me and I somehow had to deal with it.

CHAPTER 8: THE RACE TO FIND LIFE

It was Saturday morning and I had to be at work as usual. I was in my room laying on my bed still thinking about everything that happened yesterday, trying to swallow the harsh reality of my unfolding life. Who could I even tell about my struggles? I didn't want to cause Mama to worry by telling her that my hours at work were getting cut short to one day a week and that I had low 'F' in English. I knew for a fact that Julia wouldn't understand because she was too young, so my only option was to call grandma.

I got my phone and decided to call her. It rang a couple times and went to voicemail. I tried again, and still; it went to voicemail. I knew she was still sick, but I was hoping that she would pick up the phone because I really needed someone to talk to. I felt like a vase that was broken into pieces and those broken pieces breaking into more pieces. More and more of me was broken and my whole life was now shattered. To think that this whole time, my whole life really, I tried to live in such a way that would please God, despite my surroundings, challenges, and experiences. Just for all this to happen to me.

Again, the thoughts and feelings started swirling around in my head. Feelings of sadness, hopelessness, frustration, and anger followed by thoughts of suicide. That thought within my head was trying to reason with me about why it was a good idea.

"There's nothing for you to look forward to, and there's nothing you can do to get out of your current situation. Why continue to suffer when you can just end it here?"

"Nobody really cares, nobody can help. Nobody likes you and neither does God. Look at your life, look at what's going on. If God really cared, He'd help you, but He's not. So just do it!"

I tried not to listen to these seemingly external thoughts that kept encouraging me to do it. To end it all. But I was at the very end of my rope. I wanted to stop stressing, worrying, doubting, being fearful, and working hard just to see the things I had worked for get diminished. As much as I didn't want to do it, I agreed with these thoughts and started to think to myself.

"It's true. I'm a nobody. I'm ugly. I'm stupid. I'm broke. I have no friends and I'm weak compared to everybody else."

"My life ain't nothing, it ain't worth nothing, and it isn't going anywhere either. God don't like me and neither does anybody else."

"I have no purpose, significance, or value. All the men that were in Mama's life left her and I because they didn't see anything special in me. I won't amount to nothing big, and I'm probably gone stay in this hood for the rest of my life if I don't end up dead somewhere. I'll end up being JUST LIKE MY FATHER!!!"

I never wanted to go down this route but, in this moment, it just seemed so true, easy to believe, and accept. But then, out of nowhere another thought popped up, a small gentle internal still voice, came to me almost in a whisper.

"There is hope for you. There is an abundant life for you. And there is a way for you. You are great. You are special, set apart. You are loved!"

"No, it's not! Look at me! Look! Look at me! How?! How is it a way for me?!" I thought back in response to this voice.

I stood up asking God how could there be a way for me? In great emotion. Consumed mostly by frustration and anger, I shouted angrily. Thinking about Deon, Ashley, and all the people who wronged me, past teachers, and peers. In all my anger I shouted again and punched my wooden clothing dresser in my room so hard, that I chipped off a piece of paint and skinned off a piece of my skin on my knuckles while blood trickled out.

I looked over at the door and saw Julia staring at me scared. I walked out the room to get a band-aid as Julia ran from the doorway. I knew she was going to tell Mama what happened, but I was out of my usual self, and I already knew that today was going to be yet another bad day.

I went to the bathroom, washed off the cut and put on a band-aid and returned to my room. At that moment, I dropped down to my knees, sincerely, in pure brokenness and agony and cried my heart out.

"G-G-G-G-G-God! Lord? JESUS!? JESUS...Jesus?" I cried out.

"S-s-s-somehow i-i-i-if you can fix me, fix this, then g-g-g-g-go head." I murmured into the atmosphere not intending for anything to happen, and barely having any faith that anything would.

"Boy what is yo problem in here? Hittin' stuff, breakin' stuff!" Mama exclaimed upon walking into the room with Julia. I continued in that position without saying anything.

"What is it? Marlin, you my son. You can talk to me. Julia told me that you in here punching stuff. Like what is wrong?" Mama said.

"N-n-n-nothing, I-I-I'm good." I responded.

After going back and forth with Mama about what was going on with me, she eventually came to acknowledge that I wasn't going to explain my actions. I told her that I was going to work within a couple hours. Because she didn't want me to go outside alone with this attitude, she agreed to take me.

To make small talk with me, Mama asked me how school was coming. I simply responded it was ok. Since my grade for English was at an all-time low, I didn't want to give any specific details. Knowing Mama, she always had to force the issue and wanted to know basically every detail of the story. "I mean, what kind of grades you making in school right now?" I was already frustrated, feeling as if I had no hope, angry, distraught, and nearly on the verge of wanting to commit suicide. Why couldn't she just read the signs and just leave me alone about it.

I told her that I didn't want to talk about it. She looked at me with an aggressive look on her face as if she was ready to pull over and check me right then, but she kept going and remained silent. Within about a quarter mile from my job, Mama finally pulled over in a gas station and said, "Alright now, what's really wrong with you. Like what?"

I smacked my lips, sighed, and mumbled something under my breath something that I probably shouldn't have said. "Oh my God…leave me lone." I murmured.

"Marlin, uh-uh, you ain't finna just be blowin' me off like dat. I asked you a sincere question. What? Is somebody up there messing with you at school?" Mama asked turning her full body towards me.

"I-I-I-I-I t-t-t-told you, I'm good!" I responded.

"Well, obviously you not because now you getting upset at me."

In frustration, I let out a loud sigh, opened the door and got out saying, "I'm gone.".

Mama started to yell my name angrily. "MARLIN!! MARLIN!!!" I kept on walking toward my job ignoring her. Without saying anything or looking back, I continued to work. As Mama pulled off to go back home. I know what I did was rude, but it was like the compassionate side of me was leaving, and I could feel an inner savage in me arising, stemming from everything I witnessed as a child and everything that I was currently experiencing. The type of person who I always tried to avoid being. I realized, I was starting to become more and more like the young guys from my neighborhood, yes including the gangbangers. To be honest, it didn't really bother me now.

I walked into to work and clocked in. As I was getting prepared for my shift, I saw a text message from Mama that read, "Based upon what you just did, from now on you need to find another way to work because I'm not taking you no more."

After reading it, I felt bad because it just hit me that, I hurt Mama's feelings. I didn't mean to but, man, I was going through so much that I felt cold now. Even though I felt bad about what happened, I was still in a nasty mood. I couldn't come back to being happy about anything and I felt so angry and bitter. It was to the point where if someone would as much as look at me the wrong way, I could snap off.

As I was setting up my stuff to get ready for work, Bruno walks out towards the front of the back room. On his way out, he intentionally brushed my shoulder and bumped into me, as I had gotten knocked back a little from the bump.

When this happened, I knew immediately this was a sign of disrespect. He walked past me and bumped his shoulder against mine, knocking me out of his way, without saying excuse me or any other gestures to excuse himself, while still proceeding to the door. At this point, being in the mood and situation I was in, I couldn't hold the peace any longer. It was like the Marlin who I was two weeks ago completely diminished and now the street, hood Marlin took over. I didn't want it to be this way but at this point in my life I didn't care anymore. Immediately, I felt the urge to retaliate and before I knew it, I started making my way to him.

Right before he could walk through the door, I caught up to him and grabbed him. Without even thinking I swung him back and pinned him against the wall. Before he could even react, I slung him to the ground. I thought how I even allowed myself to get this far but I knew it was too late to turn back now. I kneeled on top of him and held him to the ground by holding onto his throat so that he couldn't move, taunting him to do something back while kneeling on his chest. He laid there appearing as if he was helpless and in shock as I was ready to combat any and every movement he could do to fight back.

Even as he tried to fight his way out of my hold he couldn't. It wasn't until he stopped trying to fight his way out of my hold then I loosened my grip on him and checked him about his disrespectful behavior. I let him go, keeping my eye on him as I watched him lay there. "Now, g-g-get up outta here!!!" I said to him while calling him disrespectful names, cussing at him. He pulled himself off the floor looking at me knowing that if he retaliated the outcome would be the same. He stared at me angrily for a little bit before he got the remainder of his stuff and walked out of the room.

Immediately after he left, I thought about everything I just did. It was like another part in me that I didn't know had taken over me and made me do what I had just done. A part of me that I never saw coming. On a side note, I knew Bruno, or another employee would tell upper management. For all I know there probably was a camera around that captured everything. I knew this would turn into a bigger issue and I had a feeling that I would get fired after today, but it didn't even matter to me.

I now had my mindset on pursuing another life, a life outside of an education or a job, that would bring me real cash, despite what my family thought and despite the consequences. Whether it was legal or illegal, I had to find a way to make money and survive for myself. I had to find a way to get to the money because having a job like this wasn't going to cut it and going to school just really wasn't for me.

Regardless of what I had to do. I had enough of being broke. At this point, I had become so desperate for something to happen that I was willing to go against my own upbringing and get money quick. Believe me when I say that I hate that I had come to this ideation, I hate that it had come to this, but I felt like God had left me no other option. I felt like He was turning his back on me/ Even though I heard He would never leave us or forsake us, so I didn't know what else I could do but turn to this mindset. To turn…To the streets.

I left the backroom and continued doing my job as usual every second just contemplating walking out. To be honest, I couldn't see myself making it to the end of my shift without getting fired or leaving. After about an hour and a half since the incident with Bruno, the assistant manager approached me and told me to come with him to the management office. I immediately knew this was related to what I did. So, I braced myself and followed him to the back.

When I got to the office, Mike was sitting at his desk while Bruno was sitting in a chair across from the desk as the assistant manager followed behind me.

Mike: Marlin, sit down. (Pointing to seat.)

Me: (Sits down.)

Mike: You want to explain to me what this is? (Points at clip of me doing what I did to Bruno in the backroom.)

Me: I-i-i-it is w-w-w-what it is!

Assistant Manager: Marlin, seriously?!

Mike: Are you kidding me?

Assistant Manager: By this footage you know we could call the police on you right? This is basically an assault on your own co-worker.

Mike: Is that really all you have to say for yourself?

Me: (Leaning back in my seat, shrugging shoulders.)

Assistant Manager: Wow! (Shaking his head.)

Mike: Alright, this is just unacceptable. You have nothing to say about this?

Bruno: He grabbed me. He grabbed me slung me to the grou...

Me: (Yelling.) B-b-boy y-y-y-y-you act like you ain't b-b-b-bump me and moved me outta the way!! T-t-tell the whole tr-tr-truth now! Stop lying!!! (Getting up to stand over Bruno.)

Bruno: (Stands up.)

Assistant Manager and Mike: (Rushing over to get between us to avoid a fight.) Whoa! Whoa! Whoa!!! (Separates us.)

Mike: Marlin, that's it. That's it! Go! Get out of here! You have to go now! Just go!

Me: (Staring angrily. With balled up fists.)

(Assistant manager opens door.)

Assistant Manager: Leave now! You're done! You're fired. Or we will call the police on you! We're being nice about it by not calling them now.

Mike: (To the assistant manager.) Let him get his stuff, call the other managers up front to watch him as he goes in case, he does something else. Marlin, get your stuff and go. And if we hear anymore reports of you being here causing a commotion, we will call the cops on you.

Me: (Collecting myself. Walking out while mumbling expletives about the managers.)

I went back into the backroom to collect all my things and put them together making sure I didn't forget anything, thinking about what to do from here. I knew one thing; I wasn't going to miss this place at all. I stepped out of the backroom after I had gotten all my things. I saw the managers far behind watching me as I was walking out. Without even looking back I walked through the doors and that was it.

What I was going to do after this was unclear. I didn't know what I could do to bring in income. I remember telling myself that Mama would think about kicking me out of the house if I ever tried to do or sell drugs. Or if she ever found out that I tried to join a gang or run the streets looking for an illegal way to hustle. To her, that would make me "like my father" which is already something Mama consistently preached to me about not being.

I walked out of the door, and started walking down the sidewalk, pretty much just wandering around not knowing where to go, what to do, or what to think. Nothing. I had no idea what to do next. I was out my hood. I had some money to get transportation back to the apartment, but I didn't want to go home right this instant. I knew that if I did Mama would know that something wasn't right coming home this early from work. Then I would have to tell her the truth that I had gotten fired. I didn't know how she would respond to me losing my job, the only job I had to support the family especially at a time where she was already upset with me.

I figured I would start to head home around the usual time that I would get off to keep this unknown until Mama let up. I walked down the street into a busy area in the city. I got further down the street where it was like a downtown setting with busy streets, large buildings, parks, and such. I wasn't hungry, but I needed a quiet place to sit down and collect my thoughts.

I went and found a fast-food place, went in, and sat at one of the empty tables and began to think. I remembered Grandma would always have an uber outside waiting for me after work. She would know the exact days and times that I would work each week because I would send her my schedule ahead of time. But now that this happened, I have to tell her about me getting fired too. I remember her saying that she was so proud of me because I was going to school, working, and planning on going to college to become a therapist. With all the things that had happened from the beginning of the school year until now, I knew I would eventually have to break the hard news to her.

I didn't want to be a therapist anymore. I didn't want to go to college anymore. I just got fired and had no professional aspirations for the future. I didn't know where to get another job and I didn't even want to bother looking because it was so hard for me. None of the places that I applied to in the past said they would hire me. They either wouldn't respond to my application or be irresponsive after my interviews, which would always go terribly. Apparently in their eyes, I was just some dumb negro from the hood who was illiterate, inarticulate, and unprofessional automatically making me unfit to be in their workplace.

I was losing my faith in God and was starting to come to the point where I didn't want anything to do with Him. It saddened me yes. But it was almost like He wasn't working with me to help my situation and was taking His sweet time to bring me out of this situation knowing that my time clock was running out. I needed Him now! I tried my best to stick with Him through the midst of this storm, but everything was falling apart now. Literally everything. I was convinced that He wasn't on my side but on everyone else's side who came against me. Now I would somehow have to explain all of this to Grandma after getting her all excited telling her about my so called "dreams" and "goals" that I no longer had.

That reminded me, since I knew the uber for tonight's ride was still scheduled, I could stay downtown until the uber arrived. I thought that it would make sense and make it less suspicious that I had gotten fired as I would get home at the normal time. Either way at some point I would have to come clean about not having a job anymore to Grandma and Mama.

So, I sat there thinking about what I could do to make money. At this age, some of the kids at my school didn't have jobs and still got spoiled by their parents. They really didn't need a job to make money because they came from rich families. They had cars they didn't have to pay for, clothes, etc. But as for me, not only did I have a job since I was old enough to work, but I also gave the money from that job to Mama to help her provide for the household and to help Julia with her needs. But now that I had no job, and no sure way of getting a new one, I was lost. That's when I officially concluded that I had to find a way to hustle.

I knew Mama would always tell me that if I ever tried to do illegal things to make money, she'd kick me out. But I knew that if I went hard after it that I could make good money. Probably more money than I made at this job or even more money than Mama. If this were the case, I knew it would make it harder for her to kick me out because I would have so much to contribute to the family that she wouldn't want to deny it. And this was it! This was the goal now. I had to make this work. This was my plan, my brand-new plan, my brand-new goal, to get money and get it by any means necessary. A professional hustler. I knew it was taking the easy way out and could cause controversy within my family. I didn't necessarily want to do it this way, but I had no other option. I had to make it work regardless.

Just as I was thinking this, I saw a pimped-out Dodge Charger pull up on the side of the street just outside of my window view. I recognized that car. I quickly scanned through my memory trying to remember where I saw that vehicle before. I realized that it was the same car that Jahmoni had. The guy who had stopped me when I was walking home a couple weeks ago. Sure enough, as I watched the doors of the car open, it was him and the two other guys in his clique getting out.

I watched them as they walked in. Jahmoni looked over to where I was sitting. He noticed me, nodded his head upwards as a sign of greeting, and walked over to me, cracking a smile. Apparently, he remembered me as well. He walked over to me with his clique and started to talk.

Jahmoni: Aye look y'all, this that dude we saw while we was driving that day. (Talking to me while reaching out his hand so that I could shake it.) What's good with you lil bro? What you been on?

Me: Nothing. (Responding with little enthusiasm and lazily shaking his hand.)

Jahmoni: What's wrong with you boy? You act like you don't remember me. You remember me, don't you?

Me: Y-y-y-yea I remember you.

Jahmoni: Then why you lookin' like that? You look like you buggin bout somethin'.

One of Jahmoni's friends: You look like you about to hit somebody.

Jahmoni: I'm saying the same thing bro. Like you good?

Me: I'm straight.

Jahmoni: Aw, ok. But we bout to head to the studio to do some recording after this. We just picking up some food right now though. I know we said this before and I ain't trying to pressure you no mo' after this, but if you still trying to make some money... Aye, you know how we coming wit it. Feel me? Aye but uh, what's your name again?

Me: Marlin.

Jahmoni: Aw ok. Well, aight then Marlin, we gone get our food and get up there to the studio. But if you wanna come, see what we do and how we livin' then you welcome. It's up to you though. But just know you may not see us again in person. The next time you might see us may be on yo' TV screen. But I ain't gone try and talk you into though. It's your decision. (Proceeds to go get food. While the others just stood around near me.)

Me: H-h-h-how far is the s-s-s-s-studio from here?

Jahmoni's Friends: It's only like ten minutes bro. You tryna come?

Me: (Thinking about it briefly.) Yea. Y-y-y-yea I'll come.

BOOM! Just like that, I knew I had gotten myself into something beyond me. I know I was told all my life to stay away from groups and cliques but seeing what Jahmoni and his group were capable of and being in the situation that I was in, I had to do it. I couldn't miss this opportunity. I know that I barely knew them, but I knew enough about them to know that they were who they said they were. They did what they said they did. From the time that they told me about what they did in the beginning to seeing it firsthand from Dawson and Casper showing me the videos. Not to mention the times that I looked them up on my own free time, seeing their consistent elevation.

It was evident that these guys were going places and I didn't want to take them for granted just because they weren't mainstream entertainers yet. Even though, as soon as I agreed to go to the studio with them, a feeling inside me went off like an alarm. A gut feeling that makes you feel that something bad is about happen. I felt that by making this decision, I was getting myself into something bad and it was almost like I could sense trouble ahead of me by saying yes. In addition, when Jahmoni walked up to me, I could smell a strong scent of marijuana at a time where recreational marijuana use was not yet legal. I never got involved with drugs or anything like that up until this point, but now it came to a point where I felt that it didn't matter anymore. This I know was the start of me changing into a whole other Marlin.

Despite these red flags popping up, I still chose to ignore them. It wasn't like I was going to be doing anything seriously bad anyway. They said that they weren't apart of any gangs. They had their own dreams and goals that didn't include street negativity. Plus, it would give me something to do for the rest of today since I got fired. Besides, I was looking for a new life any way and this could be the perfect introduction to it. The studio was only ten minutes away, so I asked myself what I really had to worry about.

As Jahmoni was ordering, I figured I'd lighten up my attitude so I could enjoy myself as I planned on going with them to the studio. I started to make small talk with the guys. Within five minutes, Jahmoni finished ordering their food and had two full bags as he started walking towards us. When he came close enough, I decided to let Jahmoni know my final decision.

Me: A-a-a-aye bro, Imma g-g-g-g-go with y'all.

Jahmoni: Aight cool, let's roll then.

I went and got into Jahmoni's car which was a four-door ocean blue Dodge charger with shining rims, tinted windows, and a seemingly brand-new paint job. I sat in the backseat where I saw that the interior seats were customed and there were all the recent features of the newer car models on the inside. As we all got in, Jahmoni and the guys immediately started to get out their food and get situated for the ride to the studio. As they all did this, they talked among themselves before directing their attention towards me.

Jahmoni: (Talking to me.) Aye, you want one of these burgers.

Me: Aight. (Taking the burger.) P-p-preciate it.

One Of Jahmoni's Friends: You in school or sum?

Me: Yea. I'm s-s-s-still in high s-s-school. I'm a senior.

One of Jahmoni's Friends: Oh ok. You know what you wanna do after that? Oh, by the way, my name Montrell. And that's Dre sittin over there.

Me: Man, I-I-I-I don't e-e-even know.

Montrell: Yea I feel you. I been there before. But aye, look at me now, I'm young and getting to the money.

After small talk while snacking on some of the food that Jahmoni bought, we pulled off and started to make our way to the studio. Jahmoni started to play some of his music and then proceeded to tell me that the particular song that he was playing was a song that he had wrote and recorded himself. As the song played, his friends began to recite the lyrics, which were pretty catchy. They started to get what we would call "turnt up" or "lit". While they were turning up, I notice Montrell reach into the gap of the seat and pull out a bag of something. I looked closely into the bag and saw that they were pills. I watched him dump out a couple of pills knowing that they were pills to get high.

I didn't know how to feel about this, but I went along with it without saying anything. Jahmoni then asked me if I smoked or did drugs or anything and I simply told him no.

That's when I saw Montrell pop the pills into his mouth and asked me if I wanted to try one. Again, I responded no. At this point, I became a little uncomfortable and the feeling that I made a bad decision still dwindled inside of me. As this feeling continued to linger, Jahmoni told me that in addition to dancing they also rapped and made music. He began to tell me that they filmed their own videos as well as edit, promote, monitor them, and so forth.

He began to tell me about how they were always working on their craft. Because they were busy trying to edit their videos as well as promote and market their brand amongst other things, they wanted someone familiar and trustworthy to help. In addition to taking care of other "business" for them. He described them as being independent artists and performers but in need of someone to handle the tougher business for them so they could focus on their work, like a manager. According to Jahmoni, that's where I apparently come in:

Jahmoni: (Turns music down.) Aye look lil bro, I rock with you. You a real cool dude feel me. I noticed that when we pulled up on you on the street. I don't know what it is, but it's just sum' about you bro, sum' different that I ain't seen in a long time. When the three of us came together it was the same thing with them, we all saw it in each other. Which is why we a

183

group, feel me. Nobody else, just us. We family we all we got. Now I don't really like people that much, so you know I wouldn't offer this to just anybody. But you lil bro, you'd probably be the only person I'd ask to be a part of something like this.

Me: I a-a-a-appreciate that man b-b-b-but what y'all want from me?

Jahmoni: Exactly what I just said. Look, if you were to join up with us, and do all our little business stuff and really work, you wouldn't be lackin' in nothing bro. Swear. Everything we get we share it with each other. We brothers. Ain't that right y'all.

Jahmoni's Friends: Yea man.

Montrell: Aye, he ain't lying man. Look bro, I ain't have no daddy. My mama ain't never really been there fo' me. She…she gave up on me cuz, for real. Like she love drinkin', gettin' high, and being a lil side piece to these other negros out here more than me bro. This is the most I ever felt part of a family in my life. So, when he say that we family, believe that.

Dre: Yea, my daddy be in and out of my life, tryna' have a relationship with me. He wasn't there when I was young but now, he wanna be in my life now that he see I'm part of something like this. And my Mama, tuh…Shawty couldn't even get me a biscuit she ain't care. Grandma raise me, but she old she tryna control what I do and stuff. Always telling me she gone kick me out.

Jahmoni: See, we all got the same type of story. My momma kicked me out at sixteen for being a hard head but really, I just wasn't going to let her force a life on me I ain't wanna live, tryna make me into some church boy. I had no place to go no place to really eat. Slept at homeless places. I dropped outta school man. High-School. I went to go live with my cousins who was bangin' but I didn't want that stuff. I never did that with them. But I started dancing to cope and making music. Now people be hitting me up to do shows, performances, all of that stuff. We live at my cousins still though. They be doing they little thang they cool. But we all bought this car, us and my cousins, we getting paid to do all kind of stuff now, our YouTube going crazy man and we just getting started.

Me: I-I-I-I just got f-f-f-f-fired from my b-b-bogus job. Just today. My Mama is g-g-g-good, but now she getting m-m-m-more strict. My daddy in jail, b-b-b-been in there all my life. W-w-w-w-we be struggling. I'm dang-near close t-t-t-t-to flunking outta school. I need sum like this man to b-b-b-b-be honest. You know what, say n-n-n-no more man, I'm with y'all bro. W-w-w-whatever y'all need.

Jahmoni: Alright cool bro. Welcome to the team man.

Jahmoni's Friends: (Montrell) Welcome to our squad bro. We got you. (Dre) I promise you we got you bro. We gone take care of you.

As they said this we pulled into the studio. We all got out of the car and walked in. When we walked in, Jahmoni and his clique greeted the producer and introduced me to him. He told him about how he met me, how cool I was, and that I would now be a part of their clique. As they did that, I saw an attractive, dark-skinned woman with long straightened hair and fit body type walk out from behind one of the doors greeting Jahmoni and his clique. "Marlin, this Quisha, she gone be a feature on a few of our songs." Jahmoni said introducing me to her. "Hey! How are you?" She responded back to me reaching out to shake my hand. "I-I-I-I-I-I'm good." I responded being a little nervous, taken away by her looks.

As they got started, I saw Montrell start to prepare more drugs and take them. The producer started to play music as Jahmoni got right to work recording. He started to record a song glorifying the street life, shooting others, killing, doing drugs, and the like. While his clique cheered him on and

186

Quisha sat on her phone lightly nodding her head to the music. I also saw Dre approach Quisha and flirt with her telling her how nice her body was, and how pretty she was. Quisha laughed as Dre got closer continuing to flirt as Montrell followed and did the same.

At this point, I really started to feel uncomfortable. I didn't like or agree with the lyrics that Jahmoni was rapping. My whole life I tried to keep my mind focused on positive things. I thought by doing this it would be an enjoyable experience which to some extent, it was. I was with new people for once. People who actually made me feel like someone. People who made me feel better about my situation. It gave some closure to what I'd be doing in the future to sustain myself. But something about this whole experience just didn't sit right with me.

I felt like I didn't belong again even though I was welcomed. I didn't know what to do. I thought that by doing this it would make me feel better and I know I was saying so much stuff earlier about finding a way to get more money despite it being in a good or bad way. This supposedly was the "good way", but I still had a bad feeling about it. No matter how hard I tried to ignore it, the feeling kept staying there, and even increasing. I made this decision thinking that God gave up on me. But now I had a sense that this feeling was Him saying that this is not my calling and I had more potential than this.

But at the same time, it felt good too. It was hard to explain. I felt cool, accepted for once, but it came at a price. Suddenly I remembered that the uber for tonight was still set to be scheduled for when I got off work and only Grandma would be able to cancel it. I knew that if I didn't show up for the ride that Grandma would get penalized, and I didn't want that to happen. I was ten minutes away from the pickup destination and I knew that I would have to catch the ride by my old job at the time they would be closing. God forbid if I were to wait for it, they could see me and that would be a problem all over again. I thought about what I could do to get home. Should I take the risk and get an uber or just ask Jahmoni and have them drop me off at home?

After pondering, I figured I would make up an excuse to tell Grandma that I found a better way home and she could cancel the ride now so that she wouldn't get fined for me not showing up later. I chose right then to just have Jahmoni and them take me home as I didn't want the managers to see me and tempt them to call the cops on me if I were to wait. I already had in my mind that I wasn't going to go back to that place ever. Just as I was thinking, Montrell and Dre called me over to join their convo with Quisha. I walked over and they asked me how attractive I thought that Quisha was on a scale of one to ten. I answered ten and she responded by laughing and saying, "Thank you! Why you look so nervous? Loosen up. Relax. You wanna sit next to me? C'mon! Here." Quisha said to me as she pulled up another roller chair. "Sit down. I don't bite." She added.

"Yo Dre, it's yo' turn bruh! Get in that booth boy!" Jahmoni said as he walked out the recording room. I sat down next to Quisha feeling happy, guilty, uneasy, and all other sorts of emotions. "Uh oh, lil homie already getting the baddies. I see you Marlin boy!" I laughed and proceeded to ask Jahmoni if he could give me a ride home later. He told me yes, "I got you." as he went over to the producer to listen to his track. Quisha leaned over in her seat to rest her arm on my shoulder while she continued to talk to Montrell.

It was like a feeling of artificial relief came over me. I stopped worrying about the things that I knew that I should be worried about. They all made me feel welcomed and accepted. The way Quisha received me made me feel like I was having an outer body experience as I never really had a female of this caliber respond to me in this way. But I knew it was just too good to be true. It had to be a string attached somewhere to this whole experience.

But the more I sat contently, the less nervous and uneasy I felt. Jahmoni was telling me different things about recording and the process of it. Quisha nicely asked me questions about myself, making me feel more comfortable, and Montrell and Dre took turns switching at the booth. Jahmoni also began to dance to their music, and it entertained me. All these things entertained me so much so that I forgot all about my situation. That I had gotten fired, that I had low grades, and that Mama was still upset with me. Sooner than later, it was to the point where I was fully enjoying myself and didn't want the day to end.

After about two hours of recording, I got a phone call from Grandma. I looked at the phone and knew that I had to answer it as I forgot to make the phone call earlier to tell Grandma to cancel the ride. I stepped outside to take the call.

Me: (Picking up phone.) H-h-h-hey Grandma.

Grandma: Hey baby, how you doing? (In a hoarse sounding voice.)

Me: I'm good.

Grandma: Oh, ok you at work right now?

Me: (Pause with silence.) Uh, I'm k-k-k-k-k-k-kind of on a break right now.

Grandma: Now what you mean by kind of? You on a lunch break or you just had to step away for a minute.

Me: Yea I-I-I-I-I-I had to step away for minute. To, um, you know, to uh, k-k-k-k-kinda catch my wind. I had to t-t-t-t-take a breather they w-w-w-w-w-worked me hard.

Grandma: Oh well ok. I saw that you had called me this morning, I couldn't pick up the phone they were running a couple tests on me. You know them doctors, they always got some concern about you, but I'll be fine. I am healed in Jesus' name! I feel a little bit better. I still been coughing and wheezing but a little less now. They still saying that I only got a couple months to a year to live but God already is saying that it's not my time to go. Oh, which reminds me, I been praying for you Marlin and God showed some things about you…

Me: (Dead Silent.)

Grandma: You still there?

Me: Yea, I-I-I'm here. B-b-b-but what about me M-m-ma. W-w-w-what did God show you?

Grandma: Listen baby, I know you been going through a hard time. You've been struggling trying to find what you're really called to do. You've been thinking if the things you've done out of the love for God are really going to make a difference, but sweetheart, God has seen it and He hasn't forgotten. He hasn't left you baby, he's right by your side. You've been toiling but now it's your time. It's here! There's value beyond your visuals, like I keep telling you, and it's greater than you think. So please, don't give up. God's embracing you even though I know you don't think you're worthy or qualified. This is what He wanted me to tell you.

Me: (Responding plainly, unenthusiastically, and with little belief.) Th-th-th-thanks Grandma. B-b-b-but I k-k-k-kind of have to get back t-t-to what I was doing s-s-s-so…

Grandma: Oh ok, alright then baby I'll talk to you later then.

Me: Oh wait, wait, w-w-w-w-wait, Grandma…

Grandma: What's that baby?

Me: You d-d-d-didn't p-p-p-pay for the uber yet, did you.

Grandma: No why?

Me: W-w-w-well I got a friend that I-I-I-I met from work th-th-th-that s-s-s-said he could take m-m-me home now.

Grandma: (After a moment of silence.) Ok now, who is this friend?

Me: I m-m-m-met him a while a-a-ago. He's cool. H-h-he said he'll drop m-m-me off and that he'll be able to do it r-r-r-r-regularly. I wanted you to s-s-s-save your money and I didn't want you to get fined since h-h-h-he said that he'll t-t-t-take me.

Grandma: Look here now Marlin, I don't know who this boy is, and I don't feel right about him taking you home. It would have made more sense to have just let me pay for the ride tonight and then tell me about this another time instead of the last minute. Why didn't you just do that? It just don't make sense Marlin.

Me: I know b-b-b-but, he was really a-a-a-adamant about it. And I just th-th-th-th-thought that it was a better choice to m-m-make. But at least now y-y-y-y-you won't have to worry about p-p-p-p-paying for my rides.

Grandma: Does your mother know about this?

Marlin: No b-b-b-but imma tell her soon. Wh-wh-when I get home.

Grandma: Alright now. I would have already paid for it by now. But with me being like this with this cancer, I been slow to everything. But you be safe now and don't let them people around you take you away from your calling and your purpose now. Remember what I just told you, God's plan for you is here. (Coughing.)

Me: Ok, th-th-th-th-thank you Grandma, f-f-f-for everything.

Grandma: Alright, I'll talk to you later baby. Love you.

Me: Ok love y-y-y-you too Grandma!

"Whew!" I immediately thought. That was close. If she had already paid for it, that would have put me in a tight situation. Thankfully she didn't but this was more evidence that the old me was slipping away. I appreciated the message that Grandma shared with me and her encouragement, but I didn't care to hear it anymore to be honest. On top of that I had stretched the truth about everything that I told her. I made her believe that I was still at work on a break when in reality I had just my job for brutalizing someone. Then, I told her that a friend from work was willing to take me home consistently and I made her believe that I was pressured into it when I was the one who asked.

I wasn't sure how I was going to maintain this story but at least I didn't allow her to pay for an uber to come out now that I wasn't working. I was excited to be a part of Jahmoni's group although I dreaded knowing that at some point, I would have to reveal the truth about my new life transition to Mama and Grandma. Regardless of that, I still felt like there was still something more to life than this.

I walked back in the studio as they all continued to record. We joked, laughed, and had a good time. Studio time soon came to an end, and it was time to wrap everything up. Jahmoni finished by saying goodbye to the producer as Dre, Montrell, Quisha, and I left out of the studio together. Jahmoni followed shortly after. We all said our goodbyes to Quisha as she told us that she had a great time with us before she headed towards her car. She gave Jahmoni, Dre, and Montrell hugs before she turned to me, gave me a hug, and asked if I had a social media account where she could keep in contact. We exchanged info and left the studio heading on our separate ways.

The four of us got in the car and pulled off. Instantly, I thought about the time that we had. Never in my life have I ever experienced something like this, where I had a group that took me in like Jahmoni and his clique. Never in my life have I

195

experienced the behind the scenes of the music recording process. Never in my life has a girl like Quisha made me feel like a somebody and make me feel wanted. Never in my life have I felt so desired like this. Like I belonged, although I may not actually belong with them. For once in my life, I didn't feel like an outcast, and it was so satisfying to me.

I knew, however, that God wouldn't be pleased with this. I knew that Grandma wouldn't be pleased, and neither would Mama but, I tried. I've been trying and I felt that I had given God every opportunity to come through, yet nothing happened. I didn't want to disrespect God by turning on Him because I knew that Grandma said that my breakthrough was here, but I had heard all of that before repeatedly, yet I was still lost. I figured that at this point in my life, I had to go make something happen for myself. I couldn't handle suffering any longer. Since I knew that God wouldn't be pleased with me running with Jahmoni and his clique, I didn't want to be a hypocrite by saying that I was a follower of Him and yet going in a totally different direction.

With that thought, I thought it would be best for me to do away with God and the Christian walk, always trying to do the right thing all the time. I had so much fun today that it made me forget about all my struggles. I knew that if I would continue to be with Jahmoni and his clique, we would have so many more experiences like this. It had to be one life or the other. I felt that God could pull me out of this situation at some point, but I was just tired of waiting, trying, and fighting. I thought that it could take another five or ten years before God would come through for me and I was really in need of a breakthrough now! Despite what Grandma said, she didn't know the totality of my circumstance. I needed a life change now. I thought that if I didn't use joining the group as an opportunity to change my life, I might as well not have a life because what other options were there for me?

Right then and there as we drove off, I decided to officially join Jahmoni and work with them to do whatever they needed. I thought of them as my new family. Just as all my wandering thoughts were whining down, Jahmoni started talking to me.

Jahmoni: Aye Marlin, we gone be at this party in an hour, you tryna come?

Me: I w-w-would come, but if I do m-m-m-my Mama gone start trippin'.

Jahmoni: Aw, ok. Show me the way back to your house then.

197

Montrell: Jahmoni boy you was tearing them tracks up!

Dre: We was turnin' up today bro.

Jahmoni: Marlin bro, imma just tell you now, we be working. We go hard and if you plan on rolling with us, you got to work just as hard. It ain't always gone be no fun and games. We work. We gone have to take you through some tests too just to make sure you ain't lame and that you can hang with us.

Me: I f-f-f-feel you man. Uh, what y'all really want me to do?

Jahmoni: Handling our promotions, recording us when we do our dance covers, handling our schedules and booking stuff, stuff like that, like our agent or manager like I said. See we been doing all that stuff ourselves but now that we starting to get big, we want to focus on solely making music and entertaining. You from our hood and you understand our struggle bro, we not just gone hire some random rich white dude to do that for us, they won't even understand us. Probably try and rip us off. You see we all got the same story, feel me?

Me: Y-y-y-yea that's cool.

Jahmoni: (Turns up music.) AYYYEEE!!! We gone be rich man!

Dre and Montrell: (Start singing to the music. Dre proceeds to pull out money to flash it while Montrell also rolls up a blunt that he was preparing in the car and smoked it.)

(We proceed to get closer into the hood, coming up on the area that I lived in.)

Dre: Aye Marlin, you protect yourself out here don't you?

Me: What y-y-y-you mean?

Dre: You know what I mean boy. (Goes under the front seat and pulls out handgun and shows it to me.) This. You don't keep this on you?

Ok, at this point, I knew that I had really gotten myself into some deep trouble. First, all the windows in the car were rolled up while they were passing around the blunt as the smell of weed filled the car.

Secondly, Dre had pulled out a Glock 9mm handgun. I wasn't afraid that he was going to shoot me. But I knew that if Mama knew about this, she would without a doubt kick me out. I knew that if she found this out, which at some point she would because I was choosing this as my new life, it would ruin my relationship with her, Grandma, and Julia. It wasn't uncommon for young men in my neighborhood to carry guns, but it would break Mama's heart after all the preaching she did to me about avoiding these exact types of influences that I was now choosing to be my so-called new family.

Me: Nah man.

Jahmoni, Dre, and Montrell: What?

Montrell: You playing right?

Me: Nah, I-i-i-it's just not m-m-my thing bro.

Jahmoni: Nah bro if you gon' roll with us, you gotta have it on you bro. Bro, people be jealous of us, hating on us, and just off of that they want to kill us. Now we don't gangbang but my cousins do. We live with them. And that too make us a target. This why we tryin' to get out now.

Montrell: How you walk down the street with without a gun man?

Jahmoni: Look, none of us leave the house without one of us having that on us. I got mine at home. But at least one of us gone have that on us AT ALL TIMES! Look, if you ain't got one we got some at the crib. But bro, you need that living out here, it's for yo protection.

Me: (Silence.)

Jahmoni: Do I make a turn up here?

At this point, I questioned whether I should even remain in the car. Even though I considered them as my new family, I knew good and well that I shouldn't be in a car knowing that someone had a gun. Anything could happen. To add to that, if I was going to be with them in the future, this would be a common thing. As desperate as I was, I wasn't that naïve enough to believe that if we continued to ride around in a car with guns and drugs, we would get away with it every time. The police were always around my neighborhood and the chances of us getting caught with the gun would be likely. That could result in us being convicted of possessing a firearm and putting me in big legal trouble. Because I knew that they sure enough didn't have a license to carry that gun as nobody in my neighborhood did, it was by the sneak tactic.

Maybe this was why I was feeling uneasy earlier. Although that feeling left earlier, it came back and nearly tripled at this point. I felt as if I physically needed to get out of the car to make my gut feel better. I couldn't just sit and be content at this point. I thought about how Grandma told me to not let the people in my life or my surroundings take me away from my purpose. I knew that being with them wasn't my purpose, but it was just something to do to get me out of the hood for now. So, was it even worth it?

I was debating whether I should stay in the car. From where we were, I could walk home within a couple of minutes. But with it being nighttime, I was reluctant to do so because nighttime was when all the violence and shootings would start to really pop off. Being in the car just for the next few minutes was ideally the safest thing to do since we were getting closer by my house. But still something told me to just get out and walk home.

I thought about Julia, Mama, and Grandma. Did I really want to chance getting stopped by the police on the way home while being in this car? Did I really want to put myself into a position where I could be put in jail? Or did I want to take a risk by walking home at a time where street mischief was at its peak? I thought about it and decided that I didn't want to put myself into the position where I'd end up in legal trouble and I didn't want the smell of weed to linger on me any more than what it probably already was. As I came to my decision, I finally took action and spoke up.

Me: A-a-a-a-aye Jahmoni, y-y-y-you can stop at this light right h-h-h-here I'll walk from here.

Jahmoni: You finna' walk?

Montrell: Why you wanna walk?

Dre: C'mon now boy I know you ain't scared of no gun. Is that why you wanna walk?

Me: Nah bro. I-i-i-i-it ain't that. I j-j-j-j-just realized I had some other b-b-business to handle. B-b-b-b-but it was cool s-s-s-spending the day with y'all...

Dre: Man, don't be a punk bro.

Jahmoni: Nah man if he wanna leave, he can leave. But like I said, if you plan on rolling with us, we gone test you first. And this right here, ain't solid. First you ask me to drop you off now you talking about you wanna walk.

Montrell: Yea, you sure you don't do drugs bro?

(Stops at light to let me out.)

Me: Aight y'all, it...

Jahmoni: Aye man just make up yo' mind aight? It's either you in or you out it ain't no in between. Because if you pull some like this again, we cutting you off. Ain't no room for fakes.

Me: (Not knowing what to say.)

Montrell: Shut the door bro! Must be tryna get us in trouble or some.

Me: (Shuts door and starts walking. Jahmoni and his clique drive off in the direction that I start to walk in to go home.)

So, there I went on my way home, walking. I was on a main street in my neighborhood. Walking in the hood at night always set me on edge. The feelings that you would get. The feeling that at any moment, something could just jump off. It was like you could sense it. Hearing all types of noises and voices coming from background areas as you saw how people stared at you while you walked by, watching you.

This night was no different. The atmosphere, I could just feel the evil in it and the negativity. I walked down the street as I saw cop cars speeding down the street along with ambulances. As this went on, I began to think, how would I manage this situation with Jahmoni? They seemed pretty upset because I got out of the car, and I don't know how they would feel about me moving forward. I wasn't even sure where this would go. I wasn't certain of anything after what I had just done. Yea, they were on their path to success but what tests did they want me to go through to go along with them? Would I be able to pass them? Did I already mess it up by leaving the car? I was uncertain about it all.

Then they wanted me to carry a gun just to be around them. If I ever bought that around the house, Mama would kick me out and I already knew that if I went to live at their house, I'd be putting myself in even greater danger. Now all the talk that I did to myself inside my head about doing "whatever it takes" to survive and make money was starting to become idle. Even my back up opportunity to live comfortably that was presented to me on a whim, was uncertain, uncomfortable, and still hanging in the balance.

For the record, I didn't get out of the car to somehow make God happy with me or to say that I did a good thing, I did it just so that my stomach could feel better. Just being in that situation in the car for some reason made me feel sick to my stomach and I knew that it was God. Honestly, I didn't feel like I made the right decision. I felt that I could have just jeopardized a golden opportunity to live a somewhat decent life. This one opportunity, God just had to make me jeopardize it. I just hoped that He had something else better in mind and that He would just let it happen within the next few days, because if He didn't, then I would just be done with my life completely.

I got further through the neighborhood closer by my house. All the walking that I had done up until this point felt like I was walking through the valley of the shadow of death. But strangely enough, I felt a presence with me the whole way. A real sensible presence, a good presence and it was…peaceful. It was calming. I had walked past groups of dangerous youth who were outside on the front porch, yet I didn't get touched and they just ignored me. I walked past cop cars who were roaming around as if they were just looking to make an arrest, yet no one bothered or questioned me. I walked past people who also appeared to be mentally ill and on drugs yet none of them said anything to me. Prostitutes who walked the streets, didn't even look my way.

As I was about to get onto the last block to my place, I quickly looked down the street to the right of me while passing an intersection. While doing so, I saw a couple cop cars lined up in front of each other. As I continued to move forward, I saw Jahmoni's car, the same exact pimped out Dodge Charger that I had just gotten out of. I looked even more closely, and I saw Jahmoni, Dre, and Montrell sitting on the ground in handcuffs while surrounded by police cars. I also saw one policeman looking inside the car with the door open appearing to be searching the car.

"OH MY GOSH!" I thought. They got stopped by the police right after I got out. They were getting arrested while the police were searching the car knowing that they had a gun in the car along with drugs…?! "WOW!" I thought, that could've been me. I could've also been in handcuffs, on my way to jail. I didn't know what they had done with the gun and the other drugs, but I'm sure they tried to hide it. The way that the officers were looking in the car, it was likely that they would find it in addition to the weed which would mean a possible conviction resulting in multiple years of prison. I just couldn't believe it, yet I could. I had officially dodged a bullet, and I knew that it was God.

I went through the gate into my apartment where Mama was sitting down waiting for me. It was obvious by the look on her face that she was not happy. In her angry demeanor, she wasted no time to get on me.

Mama: Oh, so you don't answer your phone anymore now huh?

Me: (Checks phone and sees that I have several missed calls from her.)

Mama: Yea, uh-huh.

Me: (Realizes that I still had the smell of marijuana on me.) I g-g-gotta use the bathroom r-r-r-right quick. (Quickly attempting to make my way to the bathroom.)

Mama: Nah, ah-uh, Marlin come here! Come here!!!

Me: (Walks over to her.)

Mama: (Smells weed trace.) Oh, so that's what you doing now? You smoking?

Me: N-n-n-nah I-I-I-m not it was just around me.

Mama: (Gives a slight chuckle then changing into a more serious attitude.) No, you was around it! Don't even make no sense. I thought you was supposed to be at work.

Me: I was…

Mama: (Chuckles again.) So, you lying now too?! Your job called.

Me: (Silence.)

Mama: Yea, and they told me that you was up there clownin' and you got fired. So, I'm only gone ask once, where did you go after you got fired!!!?

At this point, I didn't feel like lying or bending the truth anymore. I thought that it would be best if I came clean and fully explained myself. With an attitude, I explained to her my problems at work with Bruno and that because of that fight, I got fired. Then I proceeded to tell her how I met Jahmoni a while back and that I got in the car with them to go to the studio. As I told her my story, she interrupted me multiple times adding her corrections about the decisions that I made. I told her about the phone call with Grandma and how she canceled the uber ride so I could ride home with them. Finally, I told her how I saw them pull out a gun, which made me get out and walk out and how I saw them being arrested by the police.

After I came all the way clean Mama was still angry, "I told you, time and time again, not to be like your father!!! Didn't I!? Boy you know he was hanging around the wrong crowd, doing and selling drugs. And that's why he in jail now. STILL in jail!! And now you wanna come right behind him and do the same thing. Because you scared to be called a 'lame'? Don't talk to them boys nomo. Or any of these other gangbanging boys out here or you gone have to get of this house. You understand me?"

I sighed stressfully while throwing my hands up in the air in frustration. "Now get in that shower and get that smell off you. Take them clothes off and wash them good. After this you on punishment I don't want to see you hanging outside, playing your game, watching TV, nothing except for studying, reading, and doing homework. I know them grades probably low too." She added while continuing to go on and on about all the mess that happened today. "And get to bed after your shower too! Because we are all going to church tomorrow!" She said.

Julia tried to talk to me while I was on my way to the bathroom to understand everything that was going on. I told her to just go back to bed and not worry about it. I got in the shower and got straight into bed, not because I was scared that Mama would whoop me or anything if I didn't, but I was tired. I was tired of absolutely everything. I was worried and just wanted a way out. Not just a way out of the hood, not just a way out of this situation, but out of life itself. I wanted to end it all. I wanted to be done with my life that I hated. I wanted to just be…Dead.

I wanted all the pain, uncertainty, fear, anxiety, sadness, and suffering, to be over. Really, I gave God chances, yet nothing happened. I prayed, I did the things that the Bible and other Christian leaders said were right. I tried to make goals for myself to accomplish my overall dream, even incorporating faith to help with it, but even the goals that I made failed. I was trying my best to make something of myself, yet I continue to see those like Deon and Ashley advance and get blessed with ease. I embarrassed myself in front of a whole classroom. I had just gotten fired and now had no way of a real income to support a struggling family. To add to that, now I was on punishment, possibly on the verge of getting kicked out, so hustling wasn't a smart option.

Any real chances that I had left of moving forward with Jahmoni and his dancing clique were gone, even if they did want me back. I was sure that the police who were searching their car had found the gun which meant they may all have to do time. The one positive thing that popped up in my life, was gone. Grandma was still in the hospital battling lung cancer and I wasn't confident that she'd overcome it. One of the few lights in my life, who could guide, motivate, inspire, and enlighten me, could be gone within a year. I had no friends except for one, no one to fall back on, no one to really talk to that would understand me. Most people that I knew were against me anyway.

My life wasn't going anywhere. I practically had no future. If my life was this terrible now, I couldn't imagine what it'd be like moving forward. I was broken, empty, torn apart, bitter, angry, and depressed. To top it all off, Mama was upset with me, upset that I lied to her and Grandma. I knew that would affect our relationship. My neighborhood was dangerous, I could end up dead just from being in the wrong spot at the wrong time. I saw on the news the other day how a boy who lived a few blocks away from us was shot and killed by accident. I knew that trying to use drugs to cope weren't going to solve my problems, and neither would alcohol, it would only make matters worse.

Although I understood that God helped me dodge a bullet today, I still couldn't understand why all this was happening to me at once. I had built up hope in joining with Jahmoni's clique but since they may have been on their way to jail, and Mama said she'd kick me out if I ever communicated with them again, all my hope was gone. If God loved me like everyone says, why was He allowing these things to continue? I couldn't see any turn around in my situation. What was the purpose of what I was going through and what value could it bring to my life? What was the value beyond all these visuals that I was seeing in my life right now?

I couldn't take it anymore. I couldn't and the more I kept thinking, the more the suicidal thoughts inundated my mind. There was no positive thing going on in my life right now. The only positive thing that I had to look forward to was what Grandma was telling me when she said that my breakthrough was here, but there was no sign of it. It wasn't in sight.

With all these overwhelming thoughts, I thought I'd just do it, commit suicide. Who would really care, and who would it truly affect? Everybody was against me at this point. All my emotions outweighed my logic. I didn't want to do it in an extremely painful way, and I didn't want Mama to question what I was doing. So, I thought that the best way was to try and suffocate myself with my pillow. I was tired of dealing with the pain.

I took the pillow holding it over my face and pressed down as hard as I could. Five seconds, ten seconds, fifteen seconds, and I couldn't hold it any longer. I had to let go. I found myself gasping for air. I tried again this time, twenty seconds, and still the same results. I kept trying, trying to commit suicide by suffocating myself and I just couldn't do it. I couldn't do it to myself. I couldn't even believe I was doing this to myself. I really didn't want to die, I just wanted to end my suffering. I tried one last time, and still I opted out. I just decided to go to bed, hoping that I wouldn't wake up the next morning. I laid my head down on a wet spot on my pillow from my tears. I thought to myself, I had officially lost the race to find life.

CHAPTER 9: THE BREAKTHROUGH

"MARLIN! MARLIN!! MAARRLLIINN!!!"

"HUH?!" I said in response to the sound of Mama's yelling voice as she stood from the door of my room, waking me up.

"Get up! Put some clothes on, we going to church." She added as she walked away.

I sighed stressfully, as I had obviously woken up from the night that I wished I hadn't. It was a gloomy Sunday morning for me as I now had to practically peel myself up from my bed because we were going to church. That meant I would have to get up, put clothes on, and try to fit into a crowd for the sake of trying to blend in so that I wouldn't be judged.

I remember going to church when I was younger. I remember getting up nearly every Sunday morning putting on my church clothes and having to act a certain way. But the strange thing was the last time that I remember us all going to church was nearly five years ago. Which made me wonder, why did Mama suddenly want to randomly go back after five years of not going?

However, unlike most people my age, I somewhat enjoyed going to church when I was younger. I would always listen intently with my little mind to every word that the pastor would say, trying to understand God and the concepts of the bible. It intrigued me how some pastors could speak with such power that it moved people to the point where it would cause them to cry, yell out for God, and help them get to a place of freedom. But I still had my suspicions about the church.

I would constantly see through the media how the pastors and church ministers would get exposed for using their congregation's money to receive material gain. It seemed like time after time these pastors who would get exposed would be swindling their congregation out of their money, seemingly receiving money from people in the church who needed that money more than they did. In addition to that, I knew many church going people who were straight up mean, rude, and extremely hypocritical. So, I was paranoid that even when I went today, I would be judged and witness some of those very things.

I was indifferent about the whole experience. Not to mention all the times where I saw Mama struggle while still going to church. That just added to my discomfort about going today. Despite these pros and cons, I sure did not want to go on a day like today where it felt like everything in me was still upset with God. I still was feeling the same way that I felt last night: suicidal, depressed, frustrated, angry, etc.

Nevertheless, I continued to get ready going about my normal morning routine just like I would any other day. Mama and Julia were up, moving around trying to get ready as well. I did my normal morning routine and within thirty minutes Julia and I were both ready. Mama was just finishing getting ready as she appeared to still be mad at me about yesterday, walking past me on numerous occasions giving me an angry look without saying anything.

"C'mon y'all! Y'all got y'all stuff? Get it and let's go, we ain't gone be late!" She said as Julia dropped what she was doing and got up to leave. I looked at myself in the mirror before Mama shouted, "MARLIN!!" "WHHAATT?!" I shouted back in immediate response. "W-W-W-Why y-y-y-you yelling my n-n-name like that?" I added being in a mood. "Boy don't 'what' me, I said c'mon. Talkin' bout some 'what.' You know better than that!" Mama said as I walked out the door while she complained at me about the way that I responded to her. We all left out of the house empty handed dressed in typical everyday clothes walking to the car.

There was an awkward silence throughout the entire ride. None of us said anything to the other. I could tell that Mama was still mad at me which I think is what contributed to her attitude this morning. But I was still more worried about myself. I began to think about last night and how I tried to suffocate myself, yet nobody knew. That feeling didn't just go away, I was still feeling the same way today, like I just wanted my life to end. I was concerned that tonight would be another episode of me wanting to attempt to commit suicide. I was convinced that going to church wouldn't make any difference.

After about a fifteen-to-twenty-minute drive, we pulled into a parking lot of a church. The church was a casual building, maybe about two stories high, and didn't really have none of the extremely religious objects outside. Mama pulled into a parking spot saying, "C'mon y'all.", as she pulled her keys out and got out the car.

Julia and I followed her to the door as we entered the building. We entered the church service during a praise session where the congregation was dancing, musicians were playing, and singers were singing. Apparently, the service had already started, and we were late. We went and settled ourselves in one of the middle pews. Now I had never been to this church or seen it before in my life. So, I had no clue where or how Mama found out about this church. But I realized that it wasn't the typical church that was depicted in the media.

It had somewhat of a stage like area upfront where all the singers, musicians and the podium were. It was an average sized church and there was maybe around seventy people there on this day. It didn't appear to be overly religious being void of religious relics like statues, pictures, stained glass, and those type of things. It was a predominately black church which also seemed to be a traditional black church based upon the music and dancing as the service was transitioning into a praise break. As that was happening, I looked around and watched as everybody danced and looked like they were having fun. I thought to myself how much I really didn't want to be here and judging by the look on Julia's face, I could tell that she didn't want to either. But I continued to try to keep a positive body language just so that Mama wouldn't try and check me, as she was starting to get into the music.

After the praise break, the tempo of service slowed down, while the music changed into more of a slow, calming, and relaxed sound. The background singers got quiet as the lead singer began to sing. Within seconds of her singing, it felt like a wave of peace hit the building, and everybody yielded. I looked around as people began to lift their hands and some even started to cry. I had never experienced anything like this before. It was beautiful and it came to my attention that this was the worship part of the service.

After the lead singer sang for a while, I saw a tall black man come out on the stage which I presumed to be the pastor. He took the place of the lead singer and led the rest of the church in worship. Now I recognized something different about this pastor. He didn't seem to be overly preachy or religious, but he wasn't too laid back either. He didn't have the traditional pastor look, having a priest collar or a robe or anything like that, but he was sort of dressed business casually.

After the worship session was over the pastor allowed everyone to take their seats. After everyone sat down and got situated, the pastor started off the service by welcoming all the newcomers to the church. He asked for anybody that was new to the church to stand up so that the rest of the church could acknowledge them. In obedience, Mama looked at us as she motioned for us to stand up. As we stood and everyone clapped for us, I noticed how the pastor locked eyes on me. He barely looked at Julia or Mama, just me. He kept his eyes fixed on me until he welcomed us all to the church and allowed us to take our seats again.

I found it strange the way he locked his eyes on me before he greeted us all, but I didn't care too much either because I already had my assumption made up about him as a pastor. I made sure to take my precautions before he started his message, as I prepared to analyze everything, to reinforce my belief about most preachers being scammers. I was sure that although this pastor may look different than most in his appearance, he was still no different than the rest.

He started off the message by describing how there was a time in the bible where Jesus felt forsaken. He went into detail mentioning how when Jesus was hanging on the cross, He asked God why He forsook him saying, "My God! My God! Why have you forsaken me?!" He then stated that God also said in the bible that He will never leave nor forsake us.

"Now, why would God, all knowing and perfect in all His ways, say that He would never forsake us yet...His only begotten Son pleads asking Him why He's been forsaken. And remember now, Jesus is perfect too. Hasn't made even one mistake, yet, He has been sent to endure all this pain for every living human being. And I just thought, what did Jesus ever do to be forsaken? He did everything right, was about His Father's business and did exactly what He came to earth to do." Now that he started to mention it, I too began to wonder this as the pastor bought this to everyone's attention, because I've heard of both of those things but never realized it.

"See but already Jesus knew that God would never leave Him or forsake Him. Because He knew God's word. And He is God, He is the word. So, then you would ask, 'why would Jesus ask that when He already knew that God DIDN'T forsake him?" The pastor explained as he began to transition into his next point. He said that although Jesus felt forsaken, he didn't actually believe it. He didn't believe it because He knew that God wouldn't forsake Him. He already knew the outcome of His circumstance because He knew what His purpose and what God's promise was, having His faith in that. He added that the very fact that some of us may feel forsaken may be the very evidence that our breakthrough is near. And that right there instantly just hit me. WOW!!

He expanded by saying that to believe something means to accept that belief as truth. And even though Jesus might have said that He didn't actually accept that as His truth. The pastor then mentioned about how Jesus asked God why He was being forsaken a second time. He brought up how when Jesus cried out the second time, his spirit yielded, and immediately the earth quaked, rocks tore apart, and righteous souls who were dead were raised up. According to the pastor, all of this was symbolic of a breakthrough. This is when the pastor really got stirred up and started preaching.

Pastor: "See some of you been at this spot in life, where you felt like God has forsaken you. Like He's left you or turned His back on you. But see, that's normal to feel this way in your walk with God. Even Jesus felt this way. It's not always going to be a perfect life when God's in it. But I promise you, your breakthrough will come. See it's one thing to feel forsaken but it's another thing to believe that you're forsaken. Because you know you're close to your breakthrough when you feel like God has forsaken you. Look, look at Jesus. It was at his most painful, traumatizing, and humiliating part of his life where he broke through and when He broke through, the same people who crucified him, talked about Him, and mocked Him were now taking Him seriously. They got humbled. But it had to take Him feeling forsaken, getting humiliated, getting ridiculed…"

The pastor went on and on. It was at this point in the service where everybody started to cheer and clap as the service was gaining momentum. Then the pastor finally decided to say these words, "There's value beyond your visual.

It looked like Jesus' pain was in vain. Everything He went through, there was value in it. And it's because of that value that came from everything He saw and experienced at that time we are here today. If He would've gave up because of everything that He saw himself going through, we wouldn't be able to have our faith or be saved from our mess."

Ok, now at this point I really didn't know how to feel. I've been hearing this phrase so much and now I'm hearing it at a church sermon too. I already knew that God had been trying to get through to me, yet I was sold out on giving up and giving in. However, the message that he was preaching resonated with me so much that I was beyond words. It resonated with me so much that I could barely even keep myself together. It was just so much to process all at once yet, it was enlightening.

The congregation continued to cheer and clap, as Mama did the same, I guess, to blend in. Julia sat there expressionless, as I could tell that her mind was in a totally different place. And then there I was, just sitting at a crossroad with myself. I knew for sure that God was tugging on me, even after I had made up in my mind that I didn't want to serve Him anymore.

I had been wanting to just die, end all my pain. But even after being suicidal, this sense came over me again, the same one I felt last night when I was walking home. I sat there just watching people get out of their seats rejoicing as the preacher went on preaching. The keyboardist was playing the traditional churchy chords in the background in between the breaks of the pastor's sentences. The church service was starting to erupt as people got out of their seats dancing and rejoicing.

As in a traditional black church, people were shouting and starting to get emotional as the preacher kept preaching. Suddenly, a feeling hit me in my gut, it stirred up in me overwhelming me. I couldn't hold it. A feeling building up as if I was nervous, yet I had nothing to fear. It was just that I felt like a power come over me that I couldn't contain. I couldn't handle it and there was only one thing that I figured this could be a result of...God. But why? Why was I feeling this? I thought God didn't care for me like he did others.

I didn't care for dancing and shouting as I was still feeling strange towards God. But I could still feel Him tugging at my heart, He was relentless. In frustration and confusion, I decided to go to the bathroom to gather myself. I figured that now would be the best time to do so as I saw there were multiple people out of their seats so all eyes wouldn't be on me.

I made up an excuse to Mama and went into the bathroom. I placed my hands on the counter and leaned in towards the mirror. I stared at myself, having a sense that today would be unlike any other day. I looked at myself and realized how broken I still was. I began to see myself as an individual desperately in need of help, in need of change, in need of...Jesus! Well duh, I've been calling on Him to help me, but He never showed up. But then I began to think about the message, about how even Jesus at one point felt forsaken and even asked God why? I remembered all the talks I had to Grandma about seeing value beyond my visuals, the things that I saw and experienced. I remembered the time she told me that everything we see, and experience is not always a punishment from God, but a way that He makes us stronger by building humility, making us better. I felt conviction come over me and I knew despite all my feelings, God was still there. Maybe I had been wrong this whole time. Maybe God was right. Maybe I should give Him another chance and try again...Maybe I should...No! AHHH!!!

A part of me wanted to fully trust in God and try again to live for Him, but another part of me kept thinking about all the times I cried out to God, and nothing happened. Then again, I thought about in the message how Jesus cried out a second time when He was forsaken, "My God! My God! Why have you forsaken me?", and then His spirit was yielded, and His breakthrough came. Then I thought about how the very fact that I felt forsaken could serve as evidence that my breakthrough was here. Because of course, the devil always has to try and make you give up right before the finish line. Maybe I was closer to my finish line in this race than I thought.

Just as I was thinking all of this, I could hear internally a voice say, *"Trust me! Just trust me. I will give you everything that you need that's of me, every dream and goal you have set. You just have to trust me?"* The voice said to me again. Automatically I knew it was God. After I continued to think and analyze my situation, I said, "God, I trust you." Immediately as I said that it was like a ton of bricks fell of my shoulders.

At this point, I knew I had to make a change. I decided to give it another go because it had to work. Whatever it was that was coming my way. I decided that I would give my life completely over to God just one last time and devote myself back to him and His purpose for my life. I had no idea what I was going to do about school, a career, getting another job, my family. Man, I wasn't even sure if Grandma was going to survive and how I was going to explain myself to her. But I knew that by making this decision, it would please her. It would be all that she would have ever wanted for me. God forbid if she did die, she would die knowing I made this decision and knowing that I'm serving God living in His purpose for me. So, with that final thought I decided to go back into the service saying, "God, I trust you" again.

I walked out of the bathroom into the service where everyone seemed to have calmed down a little. The service didn't appear to be over, yet a good percentage of the people were standing up out of their seats instead of in the center aisle for the altar call. I attempted to get back to where Mama and Julia were sitting. I came down the center aisle until I got to the row where Mama and Julia were sitting. I started to make my way towards them until the Pastor said:

Pastor: "Hey young man! Young man!" (Congregation looks at me.)

Me: (Stops and sees the pastor looking directly at me. Pointing at myself to confirm that he was talking about me.)

Pastor: "Yea, you. You know you got an awesome call on your life young man. Wait come, come here. Are your parents here? Where are they?"

Me: (Walks towards the front and points to where Mama and Julia were sitting.) "The-the-the-the-they over there.

Pastor: (Talking to Mama.) Ok, Mom? You're his mother, right?

Mama: (Nods yes.)

Pastor: Ok can I have you come up here? Because your son has an amazing call on his life. I want to minister and pray for him because God has a great purpose on this young man. (Mama comes up with Julia.)

I had no idea what was about to happen. My heart was beating seemingly out of my chest and my body was starting to heat up. The Pastor stepped down from the podium to stand in front of me as Mama and Julia walked up right beside me. After announcing to everyone in the church that he was going to pray for me, the pastor started to speak to me:

Pastor: What's your name son?

Me: Marlin.

Pastor: Ok now Marlin, do you know that God has an amazing call on your life?

Me: (Silence.)

Pastor: Marlin, the Lord told me to tell you that's he's seen your struggle. He's seen how you've been mistreated by your peers. He's seen the times where it seemed as if you tried your hardest, yet you didn't see the success that you wanted. Right? But the Lord says to you now that He is well pleased with you. He said that you've endured much, where most people would have given up, you kept pushing. He's seen you taking care of your mother and family. He's seen you...you don't want to be like those around you. For those around you are going to gangs and such but you don't want any of that. You want to do it the pure way. The honest way. His way. And the Lord says that since you want to do it His way, He's about to pour out a whole blessing upon you that you wouldn't even have room to receive it.

I even see, just before you came down to this altar you were debating with yourself if you should even give God another chance. And you just said, "God, I trust you." And God says because of that, you're going to see a significant breakthrough before this year is up. So let me pray for you, lift your hands.

Me: (Lifts my hands in obedience.)

Pastor: Do you believe that Jesus is the way?

Me: Yea. (I responded some with uncertainty.)

Pastor: Now I'm going to need you to believe it all the way. Now repeat after me. Father, in the name of Jesus.

Me: (Starts to repeat after the pastor.)

Pastor: I come to you today, acknowledging that I have fallen short. I fall short of your glory all the time. And that no matter how good I try to be on my own, I can never be good enough apart from your grace, mercy, and power. So, Lord, I ask for your grace today. I ask for your mercy today. I ask for forgiveness. And I confess that I need your son Jesus to save me. So, I accept Him into my heart, my mind, and my life today. I repent of all my sins and everything that I've done, thought, and said that went against you. I pray God that you would forgive me for my sins and restore unto me joy, peace of mind, comfort, and all parts of my soul that may have been lost or shattered before I came to you today. I let go and forgive all those who did me wrong and caused me grief. I confess with my mouth the Lord Jesus and believe in my heart that God raised Him from the dead. And this I pray in the name of Jesus, my savior I pray. Amen.

After I got done praying that prayer, I witnessed everybody clapped and cheered. I saw Mama literally come to tears as Julia gave me a hug. Then it all sunk in, I had officially given my life over to God. Something that I always wanted to do but never knew exactly how and never felt as if I was good enough. It astounded me as everybody just kept cheering and how I saw Mama come to tears just because I said yes to God. It was another feeling of me being welcomed like the time I was with Jahmoni, but this time I finally felt that I belonged. Without the guilt and as I had finished praying this prayer with the pastor, He instructed that anyone else who wanted to accept Jesus in their life or wanted prayer to come forward.

He asked for a certain group of people from the church to come up to help with praying. As that happened, I watched as Mama left my side to come forward with Julia to receive prayer. That's when the pastor had asked if he could see Mama, Julia, and I after service in his office as he went towards the back of the church remaining out of sight. I understood in my mind to now see this as a special day.

Now after Mama received prayer, her, Julia, and I went backstage to go meet with the pastor in his office. As we walked into his office, he greeted us, and we started to discuss what happened. The pastor began to talk to us about what I should do from this point forward since he said that he could see that I had a special purpose for my life which was still hard for me to believe. The pastor began to go a little more into depth.

Pastor: Thank you all for attending church today and thank you for being compliant with the order of the service. Please, can I ask for you all's names?

Mama: Yeah, hey! I'm Ms. Lewell, this is my son Marlin, and that's my daughter Julia. It's nice to meet you.

Pastor: Okay. It's nice to meet you as well. Now Ms. Lewell, I'd like to discuss what took place today. As I said earlier, I feel that your son has a unique call on his life. Now after his prayer today and him accepting Jesus into his life, I feel that I may need to do a little more extensive ministry for him. He meant extra prayer so that I can be cleansed further from any residue of pain, emotionalism, or hurt to get him fully set on his new conversion. Are you familiar with deliverance?

Mama: Yea, my mom was a church going woman.

Pastor: Ok then so you are familiar with that. Now is it ok if I go through that with him just so that nothing can affect him negatively and knock him off course as he moves forward with his new life?

Mama: Looks at me to see my response.

Me: (Shakes head yes.) Y-y-y-y-yea that's ok.

Mama: You can go ahead.

Pastor: Ok. (Starts praying. Older church members walk in to assist.)

After nearly forty minutes later, the pastor finished with the prayers and prayed for Mama and Julia. After the prayer, I felt like chains were lifted off me and all the suicide ideation, shame, embarrassment, depression, and anxiety were gone. The Pastor, getting up from his seat said, "Alright Marlin, and Ms. Lewell." (Looks down and smiles at Julia to acknowledge her.) "You all should be all good now. You're free to leave. Be safe driving home. May the Lord be with you all.". After that blessing, we got our stuff as we were preparing for the ride home. Upon walking to the car while getting in it, I started to think on all the events that took place just within the few hours we were there.

I went there while still trying to fully wake up from the night where I nearly attempted suicide. Walking into the congregation actually liking the music that I heard and listening to the pastor feeling God starting to tug at my heart. Then getting wrecked on the inside by a love that I couldn't comprehend. Which all lead to the pastor calling me out to pray for me to give me a sense of hope. Then lastly, receiving personal prayer from the pastor himself because he believed that the calling on my life was that important. So important that he had to go out of his way to make sure that he poured into me a dosage of life.

It was surreal to me. It was surreal because of how much I talked contrary to God, surreal because of how much I felt God had no love for me, and how even despite these things He still decided to have someone pray for me and give me words of encouragement. It was just mind boggling to me. So now it left me with a decision that I had to make…was I going to walk away or follow Him despite everything I had been through? I thought that it may be led to potential for me if I were to follow God, even though I had no idea what I could do for Him or for me, or where I could even start. Or if I should try to stick this out myself trying to find a way that I could make money just as I had tried to do before? But then I thought about it and then realized that trying to do it myself had gotten me nowhere and just added more stress, confusion, discomfort, and turmoil to my already difficult life.

I know I had said all these things about God and doing away with Him, but it became clear to me that God himself was now pointing me out to people and giving me the grace that I needed. If He did this for me now, who's to say that He wouldn't do other amazing things for me? So, as I thought that to myself, I figured that I'd just give it all up to and for Him as

I somewhat still had a little doubt circling in my mind. I decided to start to remold my mind to be obedient to everything that I had known that God said. However, I was still a bit skeptical about how my life and my situation would be moving forward. But I just knew in my head that God wouldn't just provide an aid for me like this and not provide me with something that I could build from it. I decided right then and there to just accept Jesus and follow His commandments and live for Him going all out. To do away with my skepticism of everything concerning Him but not actually do away with Him as a higher being. God Almighty. I whispered to God, "Lord God, I submit myself to you. I surrender to you and everything I do to you. God, thank you and I pray that you would lead me on this new walk with you. I trust you. I repent and I believe that you will work all things out for me. I love you and this I pray in Jesus' name. Amen" It was crazy because I never expected to go this way after all that happened, but that was my new decision, to trust solely on Him alone.

We all drove home together having a happy ride home, talking, joking, and laughing. We finally made it back home, relaxed and when nighttime came, prepared for bed. I went to bed and started to go to sleep thanking God that I wasn't going to bed suicidal, yet I was eager to see what God would do for me. I woke up the next morning feeling well rested.

I got to school and remembered how I ended my first period English class. It made me not want to go. I didn't want to go to English class considering how I embarrassed myself the last time. I didn't really want people like Deon or Ashley to see me. Regardless, I had to go or otherwise I would be getting a call home. I proceeded to go on to class putting my past behind me. I got to class on time and Mr. Wysol stood up in front of the class looking at me as I walked in.

He continued with the lecture as he gave us our class work for the day. While we were doing our class work, he asked if he could talk to me for a second outside of the classroom. I followed him outside the classroom.

Mr. Wysol: Marlin, I noticed that you walked out of the classroom when I called on you Friday. What happened? What was wrong?

Me: Oh. I-I-I-I'm sorry I-I-I-I-I was just mad at the sp-sp-sp-speech.

Mr. Wysol: Oh, and that's exactly what I wanted to talk to you about. Your speech. Now I know that you struggle with speaking, and I know that probably made it hard for you to get up in front of the class and do that. But I appreciate your willingness to do it. I admire your bravery in that.

Me: Mmmhhmm. (Anticipating on what he would say next.)

Mr. Wysol: Well, I was going to say, since you do struggle with stuttering, I decided it would be better for you to have a second chance at doing your speech. However, this time I wanted to offer you the opportunity of presenting it only to me since I know having the other students in the classroom kind of throws you off a little bit. Maybe one day after school is good for you? Sometime this week, you think.

Right after he said that it's like I got a jolt on the inside of me. I knew that this was another opportunity I could use to increase my grade for this class and try to make another attempt of getting into college. Maybe me truly giving my life over to God did actually have an effect on me for the better. I had to take this opportunity. Had to.

Me: Tha-tha-tha-that would be great, and a-a-a-a-allow me to pursue the dr-dr-dream I had of getting into c-c-c-college.

Mr. Wysol: Is Friday after school ok for you?

Me: Yea, y-y-yea! That w-w-w-would be awesome. Th-thank you.

Mr. Wysol: Well then ok! That sounds good to me. So that'll probably give you a boost for your grade for this class too. So, I'll see you Friday then?

Me: (Nods my head.) Yea.

Mr. Wysol: Alright then I'll see you after school on Friday then. Ok? Alright we can go back into the classroom.

Me: (Walks inside of the classroom.)

Oh my gosh, I thought to myself. This would be a brand-new opportunity that I was hoping for to do what I wanted to do. But I still had a long way to go. But at the same time although I was excited, I couldn't really see how my situation would turn around. How would Grandma overcome what she was going through? How could God possibly bring my family and I out of the dangerous hood? How could God put us in a place that had better surroundings? How could God provide for us in a way that we could have what we needed and not lack in things? Things like bills, finances, and everyday essentials especially since I didn't have a job anymore. Would Jahmoni and his clique of guys ever come back to attack me since they were the ones who got caught and I decided to leave while making them mad? Yet as I thought, I was still so unsure about everything, but I knew that it wouldn't be good for me to kept on worrying about these things. But it would be more helpful for me to trust that God would do the unlikely.

As I reentered classroom, I ignored Deon and Ashley who really didn't pay any attention to me today. I finished my class work and turned it in. Class was ending and as I started to leave out of the classroom Mr. Wysol said, "Aye Marlin, Remember Friday." "Yea, I'm coming." I responded. So that was that. I was happy about that. But I still knew that I needed a job to continue helping mama out with certain things. So, that was the next thing. I went on about my day, putting that thought off to the side for the moment. The rest of the day came along, I went to lunch with all my so-called friends, went to the rest of my classes, and finally the day ended.

Immediately, when I made it home, I thought about the second chance that Mr. Wysol gave me for my speech, so I decided to do another practice for it. I thought how it was always a second chance for do overs. I pulled out my speech and began to recite it. "Did you know the trouble of making one…" and I continued from there. The rest of the night came, I ate, talked to Mama about the opportunity to redo my speech for a better grade and did some studying. I prepared myself for bed, prayed, and did a quick review for my speech once again and went to sleep.

On Friday, I got up, got myself together and headed for the bus. After practicing my speech, I failed in addition to adding a new kind of prayer with it, I felt confident enough. The day went by fast until it was time to reperform my speech for Mr. Wysol. I walked into his room, greeted him, and began.

. "Did you know, the trouble of making one…" and from there I went on and finished my speech. Since this was an after-school presentation, he was able to grade it right then and there. I stayed after for a second until he finished grading my speech. He came over to me to hand me the graded paper. Surprisingly, I had a hundred on it. I also realized that I barely stuttered at all in this speech for the first time really in my life. It shocked me. BARELY, stuttering! Mr. Wysol came over to me and said, "I see you've been practicing and trying to do well on this speech. I'm glad you've did so well on it and didn't stutter to much at all either. Wow!" I said thank you in response and I walked out of the classroom being overall happy with myself.

Since Thomas has been one of the one's to drive me home, I told him that since today I was staying after school to redo one of my speeches to pick me up at the time I finished. I called him when I got outside to see if he was coming to pick me up. He drove me all the way home as we talked in the car about recent school events. Being in an extremely happy and joyous mood, I got home and had an even greater motivation to do my schoolwork. I got my homework out that was assigned for the weekend and began to work on it. When Mama came home, we talked about my speech and how I got a hundred on it today.

She was ecstatic, congratulating me, encouraging me, and commending me pushing me to go harder in my schoolwork. We talked more about how I was coming along well with school. After that, I finished with my assignments, called it a night, and went to bed.

As you would guess we were going back to same church that we went to last week and I was glad about it, for the first time ever it seemed. I proceeded to get ready as Mama told us that we would be going to church from here on out. Compared to last week, it was a great change in my reaction and my mood. I felt and knew that although being in church wouldn't justify me if I just go through the motions, but it would give me the boost that I needed to walk out this new walk with Christ as a new real Christian.

We went to church praising, and worshipping, while also listening attentively to the message. We went up for prayer and left to go home as church dismissed. We arrived home within a short amount of time. We got home and got situated. That's when Mama told me to call grandma to check on her and give her an update on my life. So, I did.

Grandma: Hey baby!! It's my baby calling. (Speaking to someone else.) Hey!

Me: (Chuckles.) Hey, Grandma! How have you been doing?

Grandma: Oh, I been good. Uh, it's getting less and less with all this stuff, you know? They said how it's just miraculously decreasing and being healed. They're amazed. And we know what that is, the prayers, the ones I, you all, and others have prayed have been working. They've said they never seen anything like this. Thank the Lord! But they're still saying that I still have a little further to go until full recovery.

Me: That's awesome Grandma, really. They can't find anything.

Grandma: Well, they can still see some stuff, you know but it's just more minor stuff compared to what it was at first. God's been working on me baby!

Me: Nice! But since you are speaking about God, I got something to tell you.

Grandma: Yes.

Me: I gave my life over to Him. I accepted Jesus! And not only that but I've been seeing things change like I had a speech that I did poorly on at first, but then the teacher realized it and offered me a second chance to redo it. So, I practiced it, redid it, and then got a hundred on it which brought up my overall grade for that class, which is something I really needed. I didn't stutter at all.

Grandma: Oooohh, yes gone head my baby! Now, that's what I'm talking about.

We went on to have a full conversation from there. After that, I got off the phone with her and took the rest of the night off sitting back and relaxing, preparing for the next day at school. The next day came along and during lunch it came time to sit with my two so called friends Dawson and Casper as well as Thomas. We all began to talk to one another in conversation and in the conversation, Casper, mentioned how he got his haircut in a predominately black barbershop for the first time.

He started to mention how the barbershop that he went to was a totally different experience for him and was in the same area that the school was in, like a block away. He started to talk about some of the barbers who were there, babbling about the barber who cut his hair and how good he was. He mentioned how he got the chance to meet the owner of the shop, Dale. Dale. Wait a minute, that name sounds familiar. Oh, yea I remember Dale.

So, I asked him about it. I asked him how far it was from school. I asked how exactly to get there from school. He told me to take a route down the main street and make a right turn, that it would be there. He gave me specific landmarks as well. We finished up at our lunch table and when school ended, I decided to head to the barbershop.

Once I saw that I had pasted all the landmarks, I then approached what appeared to be a shop a little way away. I went in and asked if Dale was there. The man replied yes. In about five minutes, the man who I asked came out with Dale. It was like a reunion between me and him as he quickly recognized me. "Boa, that's that boa Marlin ain't it? Marlin, I remember you, you was that boa that used to work at that shop I had in the city. I ain't seen you in about two or three years. How you been young man?" I responded, "I been good. Just working on some new things. I been trying pull my grades up and yea. You still own the place?"

"Yes, I do. What brings you here?" Dale asked. "Well, I got terminated from one of my old jobs And I'm in search of a new job. So, I basically was wondering if you had any openings here. Dale responded, "Whoa-ha-ho hold on now, I still got money now but not just to be throwing around, believe me I gots money, don't get it twisted, but I wanna be smart with it. We don't need that much from a cleanup boy round here like you used to be when you first started. So, I don't know what you really want me to do." I responded, "P-p-p-please Dale, y-y-y-you know my s-s-situation and we ha-ha-haven't had a chance to g-g-get back financially yet. S-s-s-s-so please don't let m-m-m-me walk out of h-h-h-here with nuh-nothing."

He pondered looking at the ground. He looked up at me and said, "Marlin, you know I love you right. You been like a son to me, never gave me any problems as long as you've worked." He added. "So, my answer to you is… Yes. All I am willing to give you right now is fifty dollars a week. You could come in on Mondays, Wednesdays, Fridays, and some Saturdays as needed to sweep up, clean, and keep the bathrooms in order. You think you can do that for me?" He asked. "Yes!" I spoke. He then told me that I had a deal. He told me the times that he wanted me to work this upcoming week in addition to telling me that my work schedule would be posted on the wall moving forward. He gave me a tour of his shop showing me all the cut hair that was on the floor, bathrooms, and everything else. From the looks of it, it appeared as if I was going to be cleaning up bathrooms, sweeping the floor, cleaning the mirrors, etc. The same as I had done before more like a janitor or maintenance person though.

Dale and I talked, caught up, shared thoughts, and the like. After about thirty minutes I decided to leave. Dale and I said our goodbyes and went our separate paths as I arranged my uber to get home. During the ride home I just sat back and pondered. I thought about how I just recently gave my life over to God and how my life was already changing. I mean, I went to the church and received the Lord for myself and prayer which shut down all my worries and concerns. Even though I still was unsure about what I was going to do moving forward. I thought about how the uncommon opportunity for me to redo a speech that I did poorly on was awesome. Now, I got a new job in a environment that I was already comfortable in after getting fired.

Did I really deserve all of this? I mean I was feeling better not worried, anxious, tired, or any of that. I felt free and overall loosed believing that whatever I would go through moving forward, I knew God would provide. So, what did I really have to worry about? All my fear, anxiety, and concern was dissipating. I thought about how just a couple weeks ago I really tried to commit suicide, was made fun of by my infamous peers, was still somewhat in a struggling situation, and everything else. But I understood that God had me through it all and He was the God of the...Breakthrough.

CHAPTER 10: A NEW LIFESTYLE

I still went to school on Monday, and it started off easy in terms of the opposition that I faced in previous times. But as the day carried on, it got more interesting. It came time for lunch, and it was time to speak to Dawson, Casper, and Thomas.

When I got to the lunch table, Dawson said it was something that he heard that he wanted to discuss. He mentioned he heard that Deon was cheating on Freida with Ashley. I chuckled lightly because I already knew it to be true from the day that I saw what I saw. He continued about what else he heard. He told us that he had also heard that Ashley may be pregnant by someone other than her current boyfriend Jack. At this point, I subtracted myself from the conversation because I understood it to be a sin to engage in gossip. Although, I wanted to engage in conversation with them and rejoice that had happened to them, I also wanted to be perfect in God's sight, so I did not allow myself to take pleasure in hearing that information. As a result, I sat back and started thinking to myself.

I thought about how since I knew this information is true, then it's just a principle of reaping what you sow that's being applied to Ashley. First, I thought about how maybe God really had been looking out for me all this time. Not allowing me to get involved with any of that. Keeping me from being "popular" from their point of view by not allowing me to get involved in relationships and such. I thought about how this seemed so crazy to me, but it wasn't considering all the things I saw them do.

The week ended up passing by and it was now Friday. I came to English class and Ashley came into the room talking about how she recently found out she was pregnant which she presumed to be by Deon. Shortly after, Deon walked into the room. "Deon!" Ashley shouted moderately as Deon came in. "Y'all, this my baby daddy."

She said to those around her who were listening. She joined herself to Deon in a hug. Deon looked at her with a face of disdain as he tried to avoid her by moving away. Class ended, and I went on about the rest of my day. I got home and did the homework that I had to do. As the night went on, Mama got home, and we started to talk. In our conversation, she began to talk about Grandma.

Mama: "Hey Marlin! How are you doing? "

Me: "I'm good."

Mama: "Yeah, well that's good. But I wanted to tell you that we were going to visit Grandma. Y'all actually gone get a chance to see her, I know it's been a while since y'all last sa her although I know y'all speak with her regularly. Ok?"

Me: "Ok, yeah! That would be great! I want to see how she's doing."

Mama confirmed it with Julia and I that we're going to visit her next weekend and rent a hotel for the weekend, when really, it would be just for one day. I was so excited. But first, I had to get this week over with. Friday came and I got home, and Mama said we were going over to Grandma's hospital, that we would be heading over there right now.

So, we got our stuff ready and took a three-hour drive into Michigan. Once we got in range of the hospital, Mama began to cry. She teared up while driving the rest of the little way that we still had left. I wanted to ask her what was wrong, but I didn't want to make her feel even worse. Julia asked

"Mama, why are you crying?" Mama responded sighing saying, "Julia, don't worry about it." in a strict tone of voice.

Shortly after, we pulled into the parking lot. We went in and checked for Grandma at the desk. We got her room number and made our way to see her. We walked into her room, and I was elated. I shouted her name with emphasis, "Grandma!" From there, we all engaged in conversation.

Mama: "Hey Ma."

Grandma: "Hey Cecelia. Hey, my grandbabies, come give your grandma some love!"

(Julia and I walking over to her.)

Me: (Gives Grandma a hug.) Hey Grandma, it's so good to see you and talk to you in person. It's been a minute.

Julia: "Hey Grandma!"

Grandma: "Oh my grandbabies. I love y'all." (She said while giving us a hug)

(Mama gets up to go to the bathroom.)

Me and Julia continued our conversation with Grandma. However, I did realize how Mama got up and walked away. What was wrong with her? She didn't want to talk to Grandma. Why not? However, this is not the first time that this had happened. Something just wasn't right with this whole situation. I remember when Mama started getting teary eyed, crying the last time we talked on the phone with Grandma. Julia and I continued to talk with Grandma as Mama came back out a little later. She somewhat engaged us in our conversation with Grandma. She wasn't all the way engaged, with her attention going in and out from the conversation. During our conversation, a doctor came in to check on Grandma. "Ok, just got done doing my tests. And...it all looks... good! Like whatever it is you're doing to get better, keep on." Ok, that was pleasing to hear, she's good and I don't have to worry as much.

Mama concluded it was time to say goodbye to Grandma and head to our hotel. We said our goodbye to Grandma and left. The next morning came and it was time to go home. We went back to say our last goodbyes to Grandma and drive home. While we drove home, Mama began to talk for once.

Mama: You know, it's a lot of past that I haven't uncovered with y'all.

(Me and Julia with shock looks at each other.)

Mama: Um, I just been through a lot of stuff growing up.

Julia: Like what?

Mama: (Starts to cry more.) I-I... I was rebellious growing up. I didn't listen to Grandma. Went out and started hooking up with boys around me, doing drugs, drinking, and everything else. Almost died one time because of it. So, I got pregnant at eighteen. Mama wanted me to go to a rehab, yet I refused and proceeded to get an abortion. I guess at that point, Mama just had enough, and gave me a warning that if I would continue in all that I was doing, I would have to leave. But I continued anyway. I ended up getting into an intense fight that sent me to prison. I spent three years there and found out Mama had moved. I got out, I wanted to go back home to her, but she had moved out of state.

Me and Julia: (Gasped and looked directly at each other.)

Mama: I settled where I could. I sobered up; I knew I had to make a change. I met a dude who had money and I knew that if I stuck with him, he would provide. So, I mingled with him and had you Marlin. But as you all know he did and sold drugs and did time for it. Then another man came along, Julia's dad. He cheated and went away. (Cries more.) Never seen him again after that. So, that's how we're here now.

Wow, that was Mama's whole story. The one that I always wondered about. Now I see why she was crying and remaining silent the whole time, never wanting to talk about it. She really went through a lot that I didn't even know. All of what she told me just left me in complete awe. So, I stayed silent for a little while Mama spoke with Julia. I was silent because I was internalizing everything she said. After a while, I decided to jump in the conversation. We discussed all what Mama explained but in more detail with each other until we made it home.

We got home and chilled out. I ate, did the small amount of homework that I had, and got ready for church the next morning. I got my clothes together and went to bed. We arrived at church, and it was time for the pastor to start the service. But instead of preaching, he said that he felt that God told him to have a testimony service. He said he felt led to just allow people to talk about all they've been through and how God brought them out. The pastor decided to let one of the church members go first.

Meanwhile, I stood back and watched. I thought about how I could get up and share my testimony, my story of what God did for me. The first person shared and after, another person went up as I sat contemplating whether I should go up while watching the ones who did share get excited and even started to preach a little. It was like I wanted to get up and share but, I didn't. I was nervous and scared that I would stutter. But was this nervousness even worth being compared to the worry of sharing my testimony? I continued to think in my mind what I would do. Then, I felt a sudden desire come over me to go up. That was when I decided that I would stop being afraid and go up to testify about all that Christ had done for me. So, I waited until the young lady got finished. After she finished, the pastor took the microphone back.

He asked if there was anybody else willing to share their testimony today. I hesitated to go up for a quick second. But something in me wouldn't let me or allow me to sit back in this moment anymore. So, I told Mama that I had to go up there to share what God had done for me and I told her that with urgency. Mama looked at me in shock and amazement, but she still told me that I could. The pastor asked if anyone else wanted to testify and held out the microphone out. I looked at Mama to signify that I was about to go up and speak and she nodded at me.

I placed my hand on the microphone to let the pastor know that I was going to go next. Remembering me, he looked at me, smiled, and gave me the microphone.

Me: Now, I'm sure most of y'all remember me from a couple weeks ago. I was saved at this church. But I have a story to tell. (Just as I said that I saw Mama pull out her phone and start recording.) When I grew up, it was hard. It was only me and my Ma at first. We did struggle, we seemed to always be last. We did always have to go without the things that it seemed like other kids had naturally. But I grew up and got older, and it continued. I go to Oaksenville High School where everything is fast, luxurious, proper, nice, and neat. Yet here I am from the ghetto trying to fit in with a bunch of spoiled kids, but I push through it all. I got picked on multiple times, made fun of, had bad grades, struggled to find out who I was and where I would go. Barely being able to find a decent job. Feeling scared for my future ahead of me, and yet I still don't know what's going to happen in my future, if I would get shot or what. I got fired from my last job because I had issues with a guy who had a target on my back and then after I got fired it got worse.

Then I started wondering if I should join with a certain clique. I met a clique of guys from my neighborhood who were rappers and entertainers. They asked me to be a part of their clique and later, I agreed. They took me to a studio, and I saw all different kinds of new things that weren't necessarily good. They ended up taking me home and asked if I wanted a smoke.

I told them no saying that I don't smoke. After a while, I got out of the car because one of them had pulled out a gun and started encouraging me to carry one as well. So, I walked home which was scary considering that I would be walking home all alone, at night, in my neighborhood. Somebody crazy could attack me or do whatever. Yet nobody bothered me, and I felt a real presence walking along with me. So, joining that clique didn't work. I felt so low, wanting to die. I even tried committing suicide one night by pushing a pillow on my face so I couldn't breathe, trying to suffocate myself.

Me: (After pausing in emotion.) It felt like nobody around me was going through what I was. I felt like there was nobody, nobody I could turn to, to give me a new better life, a new lifestyle. Mama told me the next morning that we were going to church. I came to the church not knowing what to expect feeling as if I could be judged that day yet getting wrecked by the presence of God. After that, the pastor called me out and spoke to me and led me to Christ. I felt like a new person. So, I went on about my life where I had a speech assigned that I had to perform. The teacher gave me a low grade for the speech I did poorly on. However, I went to school the next time and the teacher who graded my speech called to speak with me and told me that he knew that I messed up and was willing to give me another chance. I accepted it, redid it over again and got a one hundred on it, which of course would help my struggling grade. In addition to that, I got terminated from my job, but I found out that my old employer was hiring. I went there after school and talked with my old employer to ask if he was hiring. I ended up getting a job and with us being in the situation that we were in I know that would help. So, I had just given my life over to God, and immediately things started to change for the better. I could sense that it's more to come as well. I don't know all my future, but I'm being faithful, having full faith in God. (Handing the microphone back to the pastor.)

To my extreme surprise, I didn't stutter at all while telling my testimony. It was a shock to me. I have realized that my stuttering has lightened up over the past couple weeks and I wondered what the cause was. Was it because I would be speaking in front of groups of people like this? Only time could tell. After that, I saw how everyone gave me a standing ovation and cheered, clapping for me. The pastor started to get stirred up, excited, and started preaching on some of the things that happened in my testimony. I went back to my seat and saw Mama as she was smiling at me touching me in joy as I came to my seat. I could feel that Mama was happy with me about giving my testimony. Eventually, it was time to leave church. Mama, Julia, and I all got in the car and drove home talking about church. Mama reminded me that she would post the recorded film onto all her social media accounts when we got home.

I just sat back at home and relaxed since I had already done all the homework I had to do. Mama made me aware that she was going to upload the footage right then. The video had already gotten a significant number of views on her social media platforms since she uploaded it and received a lot of positive feedback. I felt accomplished, but I still wondered about my life in the future. What would I do as a career and not just having a job making the bare minimum? I eventually went to bed that night. I got up the next morning and went to school completely unconcerned with the video that Mama uploaded.

At lunchtime, Dawson told me that he saw my video on social media where someone took the initial video that Ma uploaded and made it into file that can be viewed through the media. He told me that it was getting plenty of views, and positive commentary. He took out his phone and pulled up the video that was posted by someone on Instagram who was running a big motivational page. Wow! The video he showed me had ten thousand views, five thousand and a half likes, and nine hundred comments, just over the night. It was really a shock because I always desired and imagined myself speaking in front of people to uplift them. That was exactly what happened in the church service. After a while, the conversation shifted, and Dawson and Casper began to migrate to the topic of Deon and Ashley again. Casper said, "Yea bro really, I heard Ashley say that she was actually pregnant. She said she went to the doctor recently and found out, that means she's about to be a mom and Deon is going to be a dad. She confirmed it because she said that she had only used protection with Jack but did not with Deon. In addition, someone heard her say that she did it more times with Deon than Jack. "Really, Deon's going to be dad? That means he would have to put his basketball season on the backburner or even sit the season out."

Deon, the guy who would pick on me and tease me? He was really going to be a dad. Yet, he couldn't do that and still be effective on the basketball team. It had to be one or the other, at least from my understanding. So, I thought on that, one of the one's who made my life harder for me, had life coming back around on him? Later that night, Mama came home and greeted me.

Mama: Hey Marlin.

Me: Hey Ma.

Mama: Yea, I was thinking about the video of you that I uploaded yesterday, because you know, I made a YouTube channel just to upload that video. I been seeing how the video has been getting a whole lot of views, comments, and likes. And I also got some subscribers from it. I also had been thinking about how you shared your testimony, the way that you did it, was like a gift. I really honor you for that.

To hear Mama, say that really lightened me up. There was something she said that really stuck with me. The way that I told my testimony seemed like, I told it in a way, that seemed like a gift. I remember saying to myself that I always wanted to be like a motivational speaker or like a pastor and wanted to have an impact on people. I recalled saying to myself that I felt God had not blessed me with a gift like others. However, based upon how people respond to the video, I thought that maybe, my gift was, to uplift people through public speaking in front of large crowds which would in turn cause a multitude of people to be impacted with my gift. With that thought in mind, I figured that, that was where I'd pursue to go with my life. My new life, to get out of this neighborhood.

CHAPTER 11: IT'S ALREADY DONE

It was Friday afternoon, and I had to work in the barbershop. Just thinking and focusing on my new lifestyle and goal. This time, my whole life really, I always felt that I didn't have a gift and that I couldn't bring any value to anybody's life because of that. Therefore, I felt worthless. But I was starting to re-evaluate myself and realize that God did give me a gift that I didn't know about until recently. I concluded that God did without a doubt have a plan and purpose for me to help others with the gift He gave me. Mama came to pick me up and we left. We talked on the way home, and I was sharing with her my new aspirations. My desire to be of help by using my gift of speaking to motivate others. I wanted to use my experiences to help guide others maybe like being a life coach, a motivational speaker, or a positive social media presence. All things that I would enjoy doing with the last two being things I always dreamed of doing.

I went back to school on Monday, and it was time for English class. I went into class all around focused on achieving my new aspirations, continuing to give my all-in school, and living for Christ, giving my best to maximize my grades. When class started, Mr. Wysol told us that he was going to hand back one of our tests that we took not too long ago that He finished grading. And, not to my surprise, I received an 'A'. I studied hard for this test as I do for every test in all my classes. I studied hard for things in the past, but I never did well despite my studying, now it became clear to me that I was completely determined to make something of myself and make good grades so I could do something with myself.

On the way home, I started to think well, if I claim that I wanted to be a positive social media presence to others, then why not start on it? Why not start a YouTube channel where I'd offer motivational and inspirational content, sharing some of my past experiences while also sharing what I learned from them? Right then and there, I made up in my mind that as soon as I got home, I would create a YouTube channel and start uploading videos consistently.

After all, Mama made a YouTube channel just to upload my testimony and got followers. So, why would it hurt if I tried? Almost immediately when I got home, I got on my computer and started to create the YouTube channel. I uploaded the video that Mama sent me of me telling my testimony in church. I went on and did my homework and studied.

I went to English class again, sat back and got myself situated. I saw someone with a leg cast on with crutches enter the room. It was Deon. "Deon, are you ok?" "What happened?" Students were asking across the room. "Yea, I'm ok. I got into a car accident. Looks like I'll have to forfeit the upcoming basketball season." Deon then said that he did not feel comfortable standing up for too long, it added pressure to his wound which made him feel like he could lose focus and balance, causing him to fall. He said that he didn't know how long it would be until he could continue to be active in that arena at the collegiate level. "Wow!" I sat back and thought to myself. Is this the man who I was stressing out about due to his mistreatment towards me? To be clear, however, I wasn't glad that he had gotten hurt and that he had to sit basketball season out, but just astonished that this had happened to one of the people that everyone in school and even I, at one point, looked up to.

I went on about the rest of my day as it came to an end. As I went home, I did the usual: homework, chores, and the like. Soon after that, I prayed and went to bed. The year ended up rolling around and it was now springtime getting closer to the summer. The holidays had past, all the school activities were starting to whine down, and we were approaching graduation time. But I continued with school as normal, being diligent as my grades were increasing. One day I was in class, and I had gotten a slip requesting me to go see the school administrators in the principal's office. I showed my teacher my excuse to go to the principal's office and I proceeded to make my way there.

I got to the office, and I saw the school administrators, the principal, superintendent, and the deans. The superintendent greeted me and told me to have a seat.

Superintendent: Hello Marlin, I presume. I'm Dr. Von, the superintendent, how have you been?

Me: I'm good.

Dr. Von: Good. Well, you may not have known why we brought you in here today, but we've heard that you have a talent or rather, a gift to speak. Since our student who we initially choose as our salutatorian, Deon had declined our offer on giving the speech, we were looking for someone else to deliver it. We've had students in mind whose grades were phenomenal, outstanding and we were discussing about whether we should grant them the opportunity to speak. Then, my well trusted principal who I hired, showed me you. I saw your videos that you've uploaded onto YouTube. I saw the video of you speaking at your church, and I must say you've had a very challenging past yet you're still standing. That's very encouraging. You're a very inspirational young man, your upbringing is unique and it's amazing that you went through all of that but now, you're being considered for something like this. We'd love to have you as a speaker in place of Deon. But you're from the city, correct?

Me: Yes.

Dr. Von: But on your record it says that you were from this district. How is that?

Me: Well, my mom didn't want me to go to school in our neighborhood since it's so dangerous. So, she used the address of one of her friends at that time who lived in this neighborhood to enroll me.

Dr. Von: Well, you know that we could have reprimanded you for that, and had you removed from our school if we would have known that earlier. But…I'm thankful that we didn't know that. I totally understand that which is why we specifically wanted you to deliver this speech.

Thinking to myself: they said that they wanted me to deliver the speech. That means they'd practically be putting me in Deon's spot with me in his place to speak for an achievement such as this. Secondly, they acknowledged the gift that I felt that I had to speak and empower. It sounded like they wanted to offer me the chance to give the speech. If that was the case, it would fulfill my lifelong dream that I always envisioned myself doing which would mean that I would be just as qualified enough as someone who had great grades and seen as good enough to take the place of the one who was seen as all-around perfect guy in the view of our entire school. In addition to taking the place of Deon, I also thought of how this would serve as a repercussion for him messing with me and picking on me.

Dr. Von: Just so that I can know and be clear, you were interested in delivering the graduation speech?

Me: I would be honored to do that. To be honest, I really don't even feel as if I deserve this opportunity, but I'd love to.

Dr. Von: Oh, you very much do deserve this opportunity. But alright then Marlin. I'll put you down to deliver the speech. We've seen how your G.P.A rose in this year alone compared to your previous years here. There's a significant jump. Deon said that he'd rather not do it because he just suffered this injury and feels uncomfortable standing. We could've got something to aid him while he stood but it's his preference. We're believing in you Marlin and believe you won't let us down.

After that, he reviewed the guidelines, and the themes he wanted me to address and expand on in the speech, but I am still able to speak from the heart. We said out goodbyes and I was dismissed to return to class. I left the office being in awe. The conversation left me in shock how they identified me out of all other students who were far more qualified.

Arriving home, I started on my homework. Mama came home so I immediately told her what happened at school.

Me: Mama, I got to tell you what happened today.

Mama: Ok, what happened?

Me: So, I was in class, and I got a note asking me to come to the principal's office. When I got there, they sat me down and informed me that they've seen videos from me and notice how I'm a strong inspirational speaker based off what they had saw from my videos. They said that the way that I spoke was almost like a gift. They want me to deliver the salutatorian speech. Also, that there were other students who had way better grades that they could've chosen from but didn't. So, they obviously saw something special in me.

Mama: So, what happened with the student who had the highest grade? Because they are usually the ones to give the speech.

Me: They said he declined. He got into an accident and is injured which may be the reason why he declined, but I believe it was because he would be too embarrassed to be seen standing with an aid or a crutch. He's arrogant.

Mama: Oh. You should call your grandma and tell her that.

So right when Mama said that I got on the phone and called Grandma. Upon greeting her, I told her about all that happened today. When I told her the full story she shouted.

Grandma: Hallelujah! I told you. What did I tell you Marlin!? God has incredible things stored for you. That's how I know that you've been seeking God like I always told you. Like I said to you, your time is now Marlin. It's now. All the good seeds that you've sown out of obedience to God, all those correct things that you have chosen over choosing the sinful things, God's going to allow you to reap an abundant harvest of success. But I'm so pleased with you son. I love you so so much. But I have to go now because they want to check on me. So, I love you and I know God's going to do great things for you in the near future. So alright, I'll talk to you later. Love you. Bye-bye.

Me: Ok, talk to you later Grandma. Goodbye.

Later in the week, lunch time rolled around, and it was time to sit with Dawson, Casper, and my actual legitimate friend Thomas. We all talked about school events, schoolwork, and our upcoming graduation. After lunch, Thomas and I got to talk for a little while. I told him that I had a note from the principal. I told him about how I was met by the superintendent. How he told me that he was told about me from the principal and saw me speak through the videos posted on YouTube and the video of me telling my testimony. I told him from there the superintendent offered me a chance to be the salutatorian in place of Deon. I told him that because Deon was injured, I assumed that's why he declined. "Yea, because he's arrogant and doesn't want to be seen like that." Thomas said.

"No offense, I know that you've never been a strong student. So, what do you think it was that they saw in you that would make you qualify?" Thomas asked. "God." I simply replied with confidence. Thomas smiled while offering me a handshake and told me that he was proud of me.

Graduation was in a month, finals were around the corner, and my G.P.A was still increasing but I wasn't finished. I started off the year with a 2.0 but it has now increased to 2.2. I was happy, overjoyed, and thankful that God had heard and answered my prayers to Him about giving me grace to be able to pull my grades up.

The week of graduation came and just like any other graduating student, Mama and I went out looking for something sophisticated for me to wear. I recently got my YouTube channel certified for monetization by meeting the required subscriber count and watch time. This would be another stream of income for me once I started getting paid and continued to upload. Through this method of payment, you would get paid from the number of views that you would get. Up until this point, I was averaging around ten thousand views on my YouTube videos. Through recent research, it is said that you could be paid anywhere from one to three dollars per a thousand views. So that would mean I would be earning a profit with the gift that people, and now even I, was starting to realize I had.

While we were shopping for my outfit, Mama started a conversation.

Mama: So, Marlin, are you ready to give the best speech of your life? Are you ready to be seen by all your peers as a role model and give them that inspiration and boost that they need? I'm sure that out of all people, you'd be the least expected to do something like this. Considering our background, this could go viral. How would you feel about that?

Me: Yea, I'm ready but I don't know how I would feel about going viral. Honestly, I don't think it would be that big of a story, like who am I to have media coverage?

Mama: Never say never. But on the other hand, I have been getting closer to God. I've been praying and reading my bible more and it's really all because of you Marlin.

Wow, to hear Mama say that really encouraged me. Gave me hope. So, we continued looking and shopping until we stumbled on something that was a perfect fit for me. So, we went to the checkout line and bought it. On the day of graduation, Mama and Julia were up, and excited for me. When Mama saw me, she was elated, "Marlin! There's my graduate. Good morning!" I responded with a chuckle. She then proceeded to ask me if I knew what I was going to do after I graduate since I didn't pick out a college that I wanted to go to. I know, I was always saying how I was going to go to a college to get out of the hood, and it's not that I couldn't go, my grades were now ok enough for me to get by, but now, I didn't have that interest anymore. I had my mind set on being something like a motivational speaker or a voice on social media. That's what I told Mama, I was going to pursue, becoming a motivational speaker and an inspirational presence on social media. "Alright now, if that's what you want to do, go for it. But what about being a therapist," Mama asked. "Oh, I mean I would still be open to it. I did a lot of work though in school to help my G.P.A this past year, and to be honest, I'm tired. I think this would be the best option for me right now." I replied.

I went ahead and got ready, washed up, put on my clothes, and put on my gown. Mama engaged in conversation with me before we left, then after doing the finishing touches on her makeup, we got in the car headed off to the graduation. Throughout the ride, I began to think to myself about the uncertainty that I once had about me graduating. Well, I proved to myself that I could. Because with God, nothing is impossible.

We pulled up to my school, found a parking space, checked in and headed to the football field. I took my assigned seat amongst graduate speakers. The ceremony started soon, and the school superintendent and principal spoke. Next up was us, the speakers. Since I was the one chosen to be in place as the salutatorian, I was the first to speak. I was indeed nervous, but more determined to deliver a motivational and inspirational speech by telling all that I had been through and how I got to where I am. Although I lived outside of the district, I came to the realization that Mama and I could get into some deep trouble if this information was disclosed. But it was graduation which meant my time here was done. So after today I didn't have to worry about going to this school. So, I was good if I spoke on my upbringing.

The superintendent introduced us all and then specifically introduced me, handing the open floor over to me. I walked up to the podium being filled with adrenaline, bracing myself, and opening my mouth to speak, greeting the graduating class, and proceeding to tell my whole life story up until this point.

Me: (Proceeds to tell my story, explaining all the emotions that I felt. In addition to all the things that I learned throughout the process, implementing the concept of the value beyond visuals.)

(After speaking about the message from the pastor, I decided to share these following words in the speech.) To believe something literally means to accept something as truth.

For a moment I allowed my feelings to gain control over me, and I accepted all my falsehoods in my mind as truth. I believed that God didn't care about me because of all the things that I didn't see coming into existence, and everything else that was going on that I mentioned.

Soon it came time for my recognition, I got called into the principal's office and they said that they had been paying attention to me and my potential. A lot of you are far more qualified than me, but it was my gift that God gave me, that I never believed or knew I even had. That's when I realized that was just one of the values beyond MY visual. Now I can use that as a testimony that would help people.

Basically, all of you have and will continue to have value beyond your visuals. But your response and how you perceive that visual will determine whether that value will come out. Because if you don't see the things, you go through as a steppingstone to the next level and you just sink down even lower in your hard times, then you won't even see that value, even though it's very much still there. You must work with it and feed it meaning that even when you endure challenges and hard times, you can still be able to recognize the negative things and get the positive out of it. Like with me, I never had a dad in my life, and that affected me but instead of going astray being like him and ending up in jail, I now use that as a part of my story to let people know they don't have to have it all to find success in life. I'm not at the height of my success just yet but when I get there, I will know it was because I chose to focus on the value beyond my visual. I can now pass that value on to my kids and other young men. So, focus on the value beyond your visual's graduates of Oaksenville and trust God. Thank you so much and I wish all of you well with your future endeavors.

The superintendent intervened, came to the podium saying, "Excuse me because I'm not trying to interrupt, but can we just give this young man a warm round of applause? Matter of fact a standing ovation for all he's been through to get to where is now. You don't have to if you don't want but I consent to it, it's fine. Marlin, thank you for delivering such an encouraging, inspirational, and powerful speech." Upon waving to the graduates while walking to my seat, I watched as nearly everyone stood up and started clapping passionately. I also saw some wiping their eyes because they were crying assumedly. Soon after the others spoke, the speakers gave their speeches, and it was time to walk across the stage. They called my name and I walked across stage, feeling like I had won a race. A long strenuous race, from the beginning to the end and now it was finished. I was feeling a sense of joy, relief, satisfaction, and fulfillment and I thanked the Lord Jesus.

The audience was released from their seats to congratulate their families and loved ones. I walked to the area where I knew that Mama and Julia were sitting. They soon approached me moving fast. I took a few steps towards them, and they passionately embraced me. Mama and Julia were crying tears of joy. "Marlin, my son (starting to cry even more) you did it. Even though I was worried about this day in the past, you did it. I'm so proud of you. So proud. Ugh." Mama said to me. "Good job Marlin!!!" Julia shouted. We all came together in a group hug crying. Then we separated and talked as they were commending me on the speech that I gave. People were walking by praising me, shouting out loud on the speech I gave and some even started to pack up and leave.

I saw a family walking towards us. Someone was with that family who I didn't really want to see. Ashley. They got within range of us, and I heard the mother say, "Hey Cecelia. Remember me?" Mama looked for a second trying to remember who she was, and then finally responded, "Hey Mia." It's so good to see you again After all these years. Yea, I remember when our kids were little they used to go and hang out." I spoke to Ashley's mother and father excusing myself walking a little way away from Mama and Julia with my back turned to Ashley. I saw her walking towards me, she got in front of me, "(In a shy voice cracking a light smile) Hey Marlin." I looked at her with a disgusted face not saying anything. "Oh c'mon. You know we used to be friends. I'm so proud of you. You're from the hood, what person from the hood can say that they basically gave a valedictorian speech?"

"Ashley, look, don't try and bypass by the fact that you literally said that I wasn't good enough for you and that we weren't friends, even when we used to be." I responded. "I mean, I was just saying... You know, like, I was just, Marlin c'mon. I was just wanting to... (sighs) Ok." (As she paused and put her hands over face.) "I'm sorry. I'm sorry. I was wrong about you. And I was wrong for the things that I said to you. It's been hard for me lately. I'm pregnant now, Deon is not good with communication, so I'm just... I don't know. But would you just forgive me, please? And we can be friends again. Like..." Ashley said to me trying to talk in a sweet voice. "Ashley, I forgive you, but no, we can't be friends. What you said hurt me, and I won't let that happen again. So, I wish you well but goodbye." I said to her while turning around and walking away as she stood there putting her head down. I went back to my family, and they continued to talk. I saw how Ashley's mother smiled at me and told me that she was proud of me. She then looked over at Ashley as her whole demeanor changed from happy to upset. "Ashley, what's wrong, you just graduated and you're on your way to UCF?" Ashley glanced at me and said, "Nothing Ma, just overwhelmed with joy and it's really sinking in." Ashley's mom made a strange face but excused her response.

After our parents finished talking, Mama got Ashley's mother phone number and we left. The whole car ride home was filled with Mama telling me how proud she was of me. She even called grandma so I could tell her how my speech went. I told her everything, even how I shared some of things she told me recently. Grandma commended me for rising to such a place of prominence and reminded me that God still had more blessings to come. We got home a little after I had gotten off the phone with Grandma. That's when I got a notification on my phone that our graduation speeches and ceremony were posted online on our school's YouTube page. I decided I'd go to my specific speech, but it had no views since it was just posted.

I sat back, relaxed, played my video game, studied my bible, prayed, and went to bed. About two days later, I decided to go on the school's YouTube channel to check for my video again. I saw that it was already starting to gain some traffic, having a thousand views. A week later, Mama stormed into my room and told me about my video. It had around three hundred thousand views. Mama was so ecstatic. It was starting to blow up. I was astonished how the video was progressing, and then it hit me, this is exactly what I always envisioned for myself speaking to inspire, motivate, and uplift others.

Whoooooaaaaa, now, this was crazy! About a month later, the video spiraled upward from there and it had reached a little over a million views. It was astounding. Mama was sitting back the whole time watching it as it got to that point. She repeatedly told me that she was so glad that I wasn't going on the same path that my dad chose. It was going viral, and the video continued to blow up. I let it soak in. I was…GOING VIRAL!!! Another week went past, and it gained another two million views, all in such a short amount of time. The next day Mama received a phone call from my school, saying that they got a call from a local news station inquiring about me whether I was willing to be interviewed for their news broadcast. All the notoriety that I was getting was overwhelming, in a good way. You know, I wouldn't let this opportunity pass me by, so I told Mama yes. So, Mama assured me that she would inform my former school to tell the news company yes.

We set up a date two weeks from now with the broadcasting team for my interview and they notified us that they will cover my story and then interview me virtually. It was a Saturday morning, the day of my interview. So, I washed up and got myself ready to come on camera. I waited for my time to be interviewed pondering about how amazing God is. I would have never expected this to happen in my whole entire life. All this time I've been saying that I wanted to be a therapist, but it seemed as if God was taking me a different route. A more comfortable and suitable route. I still haven't even applied for a college yet, and I had graduated with a subpar G.P.A, but I just knew, I felt that I was still on my way to something big. Something bigger than just being a therapist, something that would be fulfilling and suitable. Because as much as I still wanted or would have liked to be a therapist, honestly, I was burnt out from school, and I wasn't willing to put in all the work necessary to make that dream come true. Besides, having a 2.2 G.P. A would make it hard for me to get into any college, notable one or not.

The time finally came for them to interview me. I got my phone and logged on to the site. I sat in front of a camera waiting for them to come on. Then suddenly, bloop! I was on and the interviewer was on the other side of the screen. Mama informed me that she would be watching it from the living room T.V as we were going live. She told grandma the channel so she could watch along as well. First, they asked standard questions, like how it like was growing up for me, how did I do in school, how bad did we struggle, what was it like for me in high school, if I had a job during high school, how I felt about working while in high school and what my future dreams and plans were. I responded to the questions accordingly, and after about thirty minutes our interview was over. I was so overjoyed. I went to Mama's room to express to her how happy I was. I went into her room, and I saw her and Julia weeping. I heard Grandma on speakerphone crying as well, as the T.V played. They were now starting to cover my story. I asked Mama what was going on. She continued to cry and Julia, crying, told me that Mama had repented for being rebellious to Grandma. She added that Grandma came clean as well and said that she forgives Mama. Also, while apologizing for some things that she couldn't do for her, as she was also a single mother.

I turned my attention to the T.V and I saw how they were telling my story, having actors to act out the events that I shared with them to present this clip. Then Mama went silent, then the whole room was silent. After it finished and the news station went to another story, Mama cheered up and her mood changed. We all rejoiced. Mama shouted with joy, "Ahhhhh,

Marlin! My baby was on T.V, for coming forth up out of this hood." "Marlin, I'm so pleased with you." Grandma said. I immediately burst into tears of joy. As I did, Mama and Julia embraced me. "That's it baby, gone head and cry. You've been through a lot. So, you deserve all of this." Grandma said to me. We all were crying. After we got off the phone with Grandma, Mama figured that she would do something different. She realized that she had just enough money to take us out to eat. She said that we would be going to Lobster House for dinner tonight, as she brought to our attention, she had been really focusing on saving up money. So, we went out and enjoyed our seafood dinner and went home. When we got home preparing for bed, Mama came to me and brought me in for a hug and again told me how proud she was of me.

I went to bed that night overall pleased and happy about where my life was going. Just to think how depressed, nervous, and fearful I was of my future to now, being so excited about it to where I couldn't wait to see what the future would bring. It was all because I chose to say yes to God. Because I chose life. Because I chose Jesus Christ.

CHAPTER 12: BLESSINGS ON BLESSINGS

Mama and I were talking at the kitchen table as Julia was getting ready for a meet that she had in the suburbs. The conversation with Mama started to die out and we both got quiet. I saw Mama scrolling through her phone. I took a glance at her screen, and she was scrolling to check through her emails. "Marlin... Oh my gosh Marlin!!!" She exclaimed. "What?" I responded., "Look I just got an email from the infamous talk show, you know the one we would watch when you were a kid, and they saying that they want to have a talk with all of us as a family. They said that they got my email address from your school because they said that they saw you on the news and feel that they need to talk with us. Oooo Marlin, you making your school up there famous. So, it looks like they're giving us a couple of date options. They've got a time for next week, the week after that, or next month, and since this all revolving around you, I'll let you pick which date. Which one would you be comfortable with?" I thought about it for a little while and finally said, "Well, Ma you know me, let's do it next week."

"Man, another one," I thought. Another opportunity to keep pursuing after the goal that I had for myself which I planned to pursue wholeheartedly. Right at that moment, Mama's phone started to ring. "Oh, it's Ma calling. Hey Ma! Guess what! (Changes to speaker phone.)" "Nah, baby you hold up and guess, because I got something to tell you." Mama responded ok, giving her the go ahead to speak.

Grandma: Now I was just informed TODAY, that I am fully restored and healed. All my complications, gone, all my symptoms, gone. All my cells, healed. I'm feeling all around better, and I got a good report from the doctors. Ha! Now! Take that devil! I'm covered in the blood of Jesus. Yes. I will be released from the doctors today after they finish my paperwork.

Mama responds, "Hallelujah!!! Thank you, Jesus. That's great news to hear. But we also have some news that we wanted to tell you. Marlin, go ahead and tell her."

Me: Hey grandma, uh…

Grandma: Hey Marlin what's going on. I'm sorry, go ahead.

Me: Hey. So, Mama just got an email from a well-known talk show, and it turns out they want to talk to me and the family. It's just like its opportunity after opportunity. I honestly just can't believe it, yet I can because it's everything that I ever wanted and prayed for. (Sighs.) To be honest, I don't even think that I'll be going to college. Because now I just have a new vision to be an influencer through the media.

Grandma: Oh wow! But you said that they wanted to talk to the family, so is that just for you, Mama, and Julia or would it be ok if I came too?

Mama: (Interrupting.) No, Ma, you can come if you want too!

Grandma: Alright then, I'm coming. Just let me know when it is.

I gave Mama the phone back and I started getting ready to go to Julia's track meet. I walked back into the kitchen and Mama was still talking with grandma which going back a couple months ago was unheard of. My whole life really, and it was something that I'd never thought that I would see. But it was still a beautiful thing to see. So, we soon left out of the house and started driving, and Mama was still talking on the phone with Grandma. We eventually got to the meet and watched as Julia began to set herself up to run. She got in place and the gun went "POW!!" I literally watched Julia take off. Some of the others started off with the same burst as Julia did but she starting to lose momentum, but halfway through the race, she kicked it in to gear and accelerated past everyone else. She crossed the finish line, winning in first place.

A few days past, after working for a while, Dale came up to me, "Boa, I done seen you on that news, and I heard your story. I just want to say that boa you sure know that you's a little preacher. An overcomer, or what y'all say, uh… a hard body. Yea you a tough one young man, keep it up. God wants to use me to bless you. But it'll still be from Him, because every good and perfect gift comes only from Him. You hear me, keep up the good work. Yea you'll see, just keep it up young buck." I smiled and thanked him. I started to think, what did Dale exactly mean when he said that God was going to use him to bless me. What was it a promotion, a raise, or giving me some plain ole money in cash? What was it? I didn't know what it would be, but it seemed to be something exciting and something to look forward to.

Since our talk show was coming up and was in another state, Grandma decided to drive all the way from Michigan to come stay with us for that week so she could attend the family discussion with us. I got all cleaned up and mentally prepared to go and share what was on my heart. As Mama, Julia, and

Grandma did the same. We headed out and started making our way to the train station. We ordered a round trip ticket to Milwaukee where the set was located. We waited for our train to come. Now I've only been on a train once, and it was to go from out of our neighborhood to another suburb. Our train ticket was already paid for by the talk show since they were informed of our financial situation and were willing to work with us. I humbly sat back and thought to myself, I was the reason why we were all on this train headed to this show.

Of course, I had a Mama who raised me right and grandma who had been pouring into me all along. But I was the one who took all of that along with all the pain that I endured and turned it into a story to be told, paving the way for me to now have a successful future. I was starting to realize; God really does answer the prayers of HIS people who really want to do right by Him. On our way there we all talked amongst each other as they were all showing appreciation to me. Mama had mentioned how it now made sense that I went through all that I had went through because it bought me to where I am right now.

We finally arrived in Milwaukee in time for our episode to be launched, maybe like an hour before. We went backstage, to get prepped to be in front of the camera and the live studio audience, Mama, Julia, and Grandma were all getting their makeup done while I received supplies to groom myself. Then a man who was a part of the behind-the-scenes crew team spoke to me, "Hey, I remember seeing you on the news one time and I'm a subscriber to your YouTube channel. I mean I already knew that we would have you on, because they inform us ahead of time, but to have the chance to speak with you, it's an honor man. I'm a fan of your story and how you came through. I'm a fan!" I laughed and thanked him but didn't allow myself to get too excited about his compliment as I was trying to remain humble. But wow, now you mean to tell me that I'm getting fans now too? What? It was crazy that I had said to myself that I wasn't ever capable of amounting to anything significant, but now, I have people telling me that they're a fan of me. Glory to the Lord Jesus, the Most High. I let that thought sit and I pondered on it until it was finally time for us to get ready to go out.

(Music starts to play.) "Welcome, you are now watching the Official Talent talk show. Now, we have a very unique guest here today. You all may have heard of him; you may not have. But this is a phenomenal young man. So, we're going to talk with him and his family today. Ladies and gentlemen, please give it up for the Lewell family." the host of the show said.

Everyone clapped as we all walked out on the stage, sat on the couch, and began talking.

Host: So, first off let me start by saying that it's an honor to have you all here today. I appreciate it. So, Marlin, since you're the main attraction of this whole thing, what are your feelings of your recent success and story?

I proceeded to speak on all my positive feelings of my recent success. After that, I did a recap of my whole story in its entirety from my childhood to teenage years, until recently. I made mention of my church and some of the things that I got from some of the messages, and I also made mention of my barber shop. I did this all while giving their exact locations.

Host: Oh wow! That's incredible. Now Mom, how do you feel about this? How do you feel about your son developing into the man that he is right now?

Mama: Well, all his life I would tell him about not being like his father. As he said, his dad ended up in jail for dabbling in street mischief. He was always a different young man. Now he did have his mistakes and struggles as he had mentioned, and of course as a parent, I had to correct him and keep him on that straight and narrow road, but his heart was just so pure, and it remained that way. He's so caring, so kind and I believe that was why God allowed him to get to this point. I mean I am just

290

so proud of this young man because he stayed focused and strived for something greater outside of our environment. You know all the young men in our area want to be rappers or b-ball players. But Marlin, my son, wanted to be different. Though he never made it into a college, I remember him saying to me one time that he wanted to be a therapist. Now he recently told me that since he doesn't have a college in mind as of right now, he still plans to launch out and do motivational speaking. That's what I'm saying, he's unrelenting, and I love that about him. Coming from our neighborhood, that's something you need to have if you want to make it out. I believe that he's going to be the one to do just that for us.

Me: (Thinking to myself.) I remember saying to myself that I always believed that it was Julia who had the greatest potential out of anyone to bring us out of the hood or at least put us in that position. But Mama really believed it was me. Now if I heard her say this earlier in the year, I would have heavily doubted it, but now I was sure about it. The show host went on talking and asking me and asking Mama questions until he later turned his attention to Grandma.

Host: Now, you're his grandmother, correct?

Grandma: Yes.

Host: Now what do you make of all this greatness on this young man? What's your take on what he's now becoming?

Grandma: Well, I mean when he was born, I decided to step in to cover for his dad not being there. Now, of course there were some things that I simply could not do for him because clearly, I'm a woman and he's a man. But you know, I would help Cecelia out with the bills. I would keep him and Julia from time to time and try to train them up in the faith. I would try my best to be there for Marlin. He would come to me in his discouraged times, and I would give him words of encouragement, comfort, and nourishment. I always told him that there's value beyond every visual and everything we go through as people that's painful may not always be a consequence of what we've done. But a way that God uses to strengthen us, teach us, and build our faith. It's different for everybody. But yea, I'm glad he took all that I tried to give him and made something positive out of it.

Host: Wow, Amen. I'm not a spiritual or religious guy but I felt that. Last but certainly not least, what do you make of all this my little young lovely lady?

Julia: Um, I like it. I saw him have emotional breakdowns and be all mad, so he really does deserve this.

After Julia, the show went to a commercial break and we all just talked amongst ourselves as a family. As the show continued, we continued our talk and even answered some questions from the audience. After that the interview had ended, and we thanked the host of the show and the crew members and headed on our way to board the train. After we had got back home and I received all my family's appreciation and compliments, Grandma went home.

After speaking on tv, it's amazing how at both locations, my Pastor and Dale said how they saw me on the talk show and saw that I recognized both of their businesses. They both shared with me that they received some inquiries about their businesses after I did the talk show. When people called, they mentioned that they heard of them from T.V. For Dale, he said there were people messaging him about his prices were around, and that they would try his shop out. For my Pastor, he said that there were people who said that they were looking for a church home and that they were interested in joining his church and becoming committed members as well.

I found it so crazy how they both acknowledged that all of that came from me. My whole life was turning around, and the lives of others right before my very eyes. Not just my eyes, but the eyes of my family, my former school, and even the neighborhood. One day me and Mama were at the gas station, and some dudes who looked like they could've been in a gang noticed me and said, "Aye, that's that boy who we saw on the news that day." I saw them nod their heads up as a sign of a greeting and respect. But anyways, I decided that I wanted to see how my videos were doing. I looked myself up, and it was amazing how now I could look myself up and see myself with tons of views. I went to both my Salutatorian speech and our family talk on the talk show on YouTube and both kept skyrocketing in views. I looked at the comments and observed all the positive feedback. I went and checked on the motivational page on Instagram, scrolled through the comment section, and saw a comment from Quisha. She said, "I know him, I met him when the Ghetto Boys Get Lit (the name of Jahmoni's clique) and I linked to make songs. WOWW!! He came such a long way and not only that, he's such a sweetheart. (With a heart and smiley face emoji.)"

I took that as in other words, she never expected me to go this route and get so far. I felt that that's how all the others who went to my school felt as well. God was blowing my mind with all this. At first, He blew my mind because I always felt like He was never there. I kept thinking like, He's God, how could He do this to me? Just as I thought that I remembered how Jesus felt forsaken but got resurrected and set above

294

everything. Even above Satan. I came to realize how it was all based on feelings. But beyond all the feelings, there's something valuable for you if you don't give up.

The next week came and I checked my emails to see if I got any inquires as I was now becoming a hot commodity and high in demand by businesses. As I was looking through my emails, I saw an email that said, "Opportunity to Give Motivational Speech to Representatives", so I clicked on it to open it up and read through it. Basically, it was an invitation from a banking company to speak to its sales representatives. It said that they heard about me and again, saw how I was gifted to speak. It was an opportunity to give a motivational speech full of encouragement, exhortation, and tips on how to have tenacity and perseverance. Since majority of their representatives are in their early and mid-twenties and a few are in their early thirties, they felt that it would be good for them to see me, a younger individual speak on drive, motivation, etc. It also mentioned how their representatives have been kind of slothful lately and they were looking for me to pump them up using my story and gift.

I bought that to Mama's attention, and she was ecstatic saying I had now become like the father of the household. She looked over the email and mentioned that she heard of that company before. She contemplated working there once, but said the location was a little far, like forty-five to fifty minutes away. They gave us a list of dates, next week or three choice days of next month. They also informed us that if we couldn't make it on any of those dates then we could reschedule to a date that they would approve of. You already know me; I went for the one next week as I was determined to use any opportunity I could of leaving the hood.

I was physically and mentally ready to give this presentation-styled speech. Mama and I pulled up to the company on time, as they were all waiting expectantly for me. The manager of the company came out, greeted us, and gave an introduction then handed the floor over to me.

I started my presentation simultaneously with my speech. All the sales representatives were locked in, giving me their full undivided attention. When I finished, they gave me a round of applause. The manager came over and told me that I never disappoint. He praised me saying how from the graduation speech to the talk show, to just now, that I always gave a powerful speech or presentation. Some of the representatives even said that my speech presentation lit a fire under them and made them realize how bad their slothfulness was. They also said they felt a feeling of positive guilt because it made them want to do better and work harder.

Mama and I continued to talk with the representatives since most were near my age. The manager discreetly pulled me to the side and asked if I knew of anyone in need of a job right now as a sales representative. He said they've been looking for new representatives. It was like a wave of happiness smacked me in the face. I stood there silent for a moment, and glanced over at Mama, and finally said, "Uh yea, my Ma could use a new job, she's been struggling, as long as I could remember really." So, I called her over to join the conversation. He asked her if she needed a new job. Mama looked at him with a surprised look and shouted yes. He asked her about her work experience and her college education. Mama informed him that she worked as a teller and as a cashier for low wages, but she didn't have any college education. She had her G.E.D. She tried going back to school a couple times but never finished because being a mother to Julia and I was her priority. She did mention our dad was never in the household and is still in jail.

"Well, I'm sorry to hear that, the manager said. But I'll tell you what, I'll hire you to work for this company. We prefer our reps to at least have an associate in business or a bachelor's in finance or business, but it is not a requirement and since you've

worked at the bank for… wait, how many years did you say?"
Mama replied, "For a good fourteen years strong." "Ok that's
good. So let me get my application and paperwork right quick.
(Quickly walks away.)" He said coming back after like three
minutes with the papers. Mama filled them out on the spot. I
sat back and thought to myself, not to be cocky, Mama was
going to get this job because of me. If it wasn't for me
becoming who I am now, then Mama wouldn't have this
opportunity.

After filling out all the paperwork, I could see Mama
consulting to herself quietly how she was going to be able to
get from home to work consistently and on time as morning
traffic was always bad getting from the city to the suburbs.
That's when the manager, hearing Mama's whisper, said, "Oh
yea, I forgot that you all live in a neighborhood that is not
necessarily ideal. I know because of course I saw you guys on
live T.V. talk about your neighborhood and I saw it being
covered on the news. I even heard about a young boy being
killed over there. Look Cecelia, I know with your situation it
could make it hard to focus on your job, but we offer
something that would help with that. It's called E.A.H,
Employer Assisted Housing. It's basically a program that we
offer to our employees who are in need or struggling with their
bills so that they may be able to focus solely on their work. It

allows you to move into a home or housing nearby the workplace. Sound interesting?"

Mama burst into tears shouting and rejoicing. She cried a passionate cry too. She started to continually thank Jesus. The manager stood by with an astounded look and walked over to comfort Mama by patting her on the shoulder. I saw Mama then stand up straight and give him a hug, thanking him. The manager gave Mama a layout plan as to what she needed to do to get that new house near her new job. According to him, the new house would be paid for through a forgivable loan that would be extended to us for a certain period that she would have to work. After that period was over, the loan would be forgiven. Hearing him explain that I started to cry as well.

That would mean… We would finally be moving out from the hood. FINALLY!!! Something I always wanted for us my entire life and it was all because of the grace of my GOD!!! Jesus! He used me to put my whole family in a better position and then it hit me, that all those prayers that I prayed as a youngin' were answered and came to past. Wow! As Mama was finishing up her tears of joy, the manager gave her more details and a deeper explanation of the program. The company would get her in contact with a realtor so that we would be able to purchase the home through the E.A.H program. Mama got a chance to ask all her questions and soon they finished discussing the program.

The manager cut me a check for eight hundred and fifty dollars, and we headed to our car. Before we got there, Mama stopped dead in her tracks and pulled me in for a hug crying because she still could not believe what happened. As she did that, I hugged her back and squeezed her so tight and I unleashed my tears that I was trying to hold back. "We did it Marlin! We did it! We did it." Mama kept saying as she hugged me. We drove home as Mama, and I talked. She kept thanking me, thanking God for me, thanking God that I was not like my dad, and thanking God for blessing her with me.

Mama: Marlin, I'm so thankful that I had you. I remember the day that I had you. Your dad was going back and forth with the law, and I just thought, "Lord Jesus don't let my son be like him. Please." Because I knew from there, you would be raised without a dad, and you know the rest of the story. So...I'm sorry. Sorry that I didn't make it the most advantageous environment for you to be raised in. But you made it out. Shoot, you bringing us all out. The times that I was hard on you, it wasn't because I was angry at you or trying to be that way, I just didn't want you to end up like your dad. I know I said some hurtful things about him that I shouldn't have said because, I chose him. Now I choose forgiveness. So, I forgive him and just wish he could see this. He would be so proud of you. Maybe one day, he will see this, and we could reunite this family and get married if he's still in his right mind and wants change.

Me: Yea Ma, I appreciate everything you said and you keeping me on the straight and narrow. Honestly, I understood why you were that way with me. To get me to a place where I could fulfill my full potential. To get me to this place right now. Thank you, Ma, I love you.

As soon as we walked through the front door Mama shouted Julia's name so she could come near. As soon as Julia came in sight, Mama told her that we were moving. Julia smacked her lips and said, "Stop playing. It'll take a while before we can get up out this dump. (Chuckling slightly.)" Mama replied saying, "Julia! Never say never!! They just offered me a job at that place, but I was worried about how I was going to get from here to there and that man told us about how they have ways to provide employees with a new house. So, we're moving. Out of this hood we go." Julia looked at me to see my facial expression. I looked at her and shook my head yes. Julia then leaped in the air and ran up to us and hugged us, then she started bawling. There we all went crying together, again, pouring out tears of pure joy. Mama told Julia to thank God for it and to thank me as well.

It was a Monday morning after about two and a half months that Mama had the job and started working. We got our place all selected out, obtained through the E.A.H and set to move in. We had a realtor all set and Mama said that by the end of the night, we would be all moved into our new place. WE WERE FINALLY MOVING OUT OF THE HOOD AT LAST! We were finishing up packing our things together so they could be placed on the moving truck. As we were doing that, I had thought about something, I remembered that I was still working for Dale, which left me no other choice than to tell him that I would be leaving our area. Technically, I could still work under him, but I was now starting to make a significant amount of money from YouTube. I decided that it would be more beneficial for me to pursue after my dream. To be exact, I had saved up fifteen thousand dollars from YouTube since I started it in addition to my income from Dale. I brought this to Mama's attention and asked her what she thought that I should do about working for Dale. "Well, what do you want to do? I mean, it's up to you. You old enough to make your own decisions now and based upon all you've done just in the past two to three months alone, you've made some solid decisions.

So, I don't mind if you choose to leave or stay. We just gotta work on your transportation though."

I asked Mama if she could take me to the shop so I could tell Dale that I would be leaving to pursue my lifelong dream of being a speaker. She told me we would go on our way to our new house. As Mama said, we were headed to the barbershop before moving into our new house. We pulled into the parking lot of the barbershop, and I walked in to give Dale the news. He saw me walk in while he was sitting in his spot.

"Marlin, what are you doing here? You don't work today." Dale said. "Yea, that's actually what I wanted to talk to you about. Uh, I'm sorry to say this but it was a pleasure working for you. But I just wanted to let you know that I'm officially resigning so that I can pursue my passion of being a speaker. We're moving. But really, thank you Dale for all that you've done for me." Dale changed from looking at me with a serious face which quickly turned into a smile. "Well, I guess that means you don't want to be a co-owner with me. Because I was going to take you under my wing and show you the ropes of how this business runs. I'm getting old now Marlin, I can't and do not want to be doing this the rest of my old life. I want to relax. But I'm not just going to let my business die out once I'm gone, I want it to live on. So, I need someone that I can trust who is young, you're like a son to me, and you are the only one who I can say that about. I want to bless you Marlin because you are a faithful young man in everything you do."

He then began to tell me about how I was always a stand-up guy to him, always respectful, and never gave him any problems and reminded me again that he saw me as his own son since his son died. I responded being in awe not knowing what to say. He smiled and asked if I was willing to do that with him, informing me that I would be like his little assistant. He told me that I will no longer oversee janitorial duties but instead I will be keeping up on the things that are essential for the barbershop business. Things like calling maintenance people like plumbers, heating, and cooling people, acquiring all the needed supplies like more chairs, cleaning supplies, and the like. In addition to helping him with employing any new barbers by scheduling the interviews and reviewing their past work and cuts.

"So, could you do that for me? And wait, hold on, I forgot to say that I'll cut you a portion, or a percentage of my revenue too. Maybe anywhere from thirty to forty percent and then, once I pass away, I could possibly hand it over to you completely, but I'll have to see how you do during that time. If not, its ok I have other barbers here to help but you are the person who came to my mind, and I want you to have it before anyone else." Dale said. I told him yes, "I got you Dale, you can trust me. I won't let you down. I'll find a way to be here even though I don't have a car yet." While starting to cry once again with even more tears of happiness and joy. After I said that that, Dale made it even better by saying that I only HAD to be there one day out of the week, but I am welcome to come at any time and I would still have to come when he needed me. Even though I'm not required to, I should still stop by to check the place in between those times that I had to be there each week.

After that, Dale and I chatted more, and I told him about all the recent news pertaining to my family and in my life. We said our goodbyes. I thanked him and went back to the car. Mama said, "Oh well what's that big ole smile on your face for? Did Jesus himself come in there to talk with y'all. I mean, you are the preacher boy now. What happened?" I told her all that Dale said and offered me. Mama shouted aloud, hugged me, and told me how I was now the man in the family no longer just a boy. Julia proceeded to say, "Marlin, I'm so happy for you and I'm not jealous of you, you're my brother, I love you, but I just want to know, what are all these blessings for? What do you think brought them…"? "It's because He worked Julia! He stayed faithful to God and was obedient and stayed the course.

That's what brought them." Mama said correcting Julia. "But I'm so Godly proud of you Marlin." Mama finished saying. So, we went on to our new house along with the moving trucks and moved all our stuff in with help from the movers.

It was a Saturday morning, Julia had transferred schools, Mama was loving her new job, the pay, and our new house. I was still working on getting a new car which I had saved up the money for, but I also got my first check from my new position at the barbershop, and it was a totally different pay than any other position I've ever worked in. Things were going exceedingly great, and for the first time in my life I was in comfort and at peace with myself because of the Prince of Peace! I thought to myself pleasing God, even when you're at your lowest or even struggling not knowing what to do will always be rewarded. God led me back to Himself even in the midst of my thoughts of running away from Him. Even through me trying to commit suicide, He was there, and He cared. It's just like that scripture I read, that says if I make my bed in hell, you are there. He was there the whole time, for my entire life.

Through my anxiety, depression, torment, slander, fights, poverty, temptation, danger, trouble, heartaches, and breaks, and even through all my evil thoughts, **HE WAS THERE!!! MY GOD WHO I CHOSE TO SERVE WITH ALL OF**

ME WAS THERE! I got a little emotional, for like the one hundredth time over these past few months and cried with tears of joy but also with tears of utter surprise and amazement. After I got done crying, I had a phone call from an unknown number. This was no surprise to me as I was now accepting phone calls from anyone who needed help or who wanted me to come and speak.

Voice: Hello, is this Marlin Lewell?

Me: Yes, it is. Who is this?

Voice: Greetings there, Marlin. I am calling from our base at Life Coaching Training Program Online in Missouri. I was calling because, of course as you probably already know, you're a hot commodity and you've really impacted lives, even my life to say the truth. But we wanted to offer you a scholarship to go through our training program to become a certified life coach. All you have to do is fill out our application and we will be notified that you were offered a scholarship to enroll into our course. All we need from you is your consent and your filled out application. Sounds sweet, doesn't it? You think that you'll be interested or able to partake in this course? We've had some successful life coaches come out from this program.

Me: (Thinking to myself.) Now I know being a life coach is somewhat similar to being a therapist which is what I wanted to do since high school because I would get to talk to people about their dreams and inspire them by giving them advice on how to achieve their dreams while making them set appropriate goals for themselves to get there. Plus, I would be practically getting paid to do the same work as a therapist without having to go through the needed requirements of a college degree and having to pass tests and exams. And it would be my very own business which nobody would have control over except for me. For me, this was way better than becoming a therapist. So, I thought, this is God literally granting me another desire of my heart. I thought about how everything was falling into place perfectly like I always wanted it to. So, I figured that I'd just bring the phone to Mama so she could hear this conversation.

Me: (Speaking back to the lady.) Ok, Ma'am would you mind just holding on for a second, I want my Ma to hear this.

Voice: Ok that's fine, no problem.

So, I went and found Mama in our new house which of course was far larger than our old apartment and gave her the phone. The lady repeated everything that she told me, and Mama simply asked where I could fill out the application. She instructed me to go to their website as she gave me the website address to fill it out there. After that she asked if we had any more questions and we responded no but asked if we could have her as a contact for future references for questions that may come up. She gave us the specific place to reach out to her on the website.

Mama congratulated me for achieving a scholarship to their training program praising and thanking Jesus for it. I went back into my room and started to ponder. I remembered the time where all I could do is sit back and ponder about all the things that were going wrong in my life and wondered why God even created me and why He would create me to go through all of that thinking that it was all for His amusement. But now it was almost like a symmetrical situation but on the other side, the prosperous side. Now I was wondering about how all these blessing was flowing in, and I realized that God toughened me making me strong enough and mature enough to receive all that He was blessing me with now. That I may be able to handle it properly and appreciate it more. Because just being in that state of mind while we were in the hood at the time wouldn't make me sufficient to handle all of this. It was all on God's perfect divine time.

That's when Mama came back and walked into my room sitting down on my bed. She talked with me for a little bit and got up to walk out of my room but before she left out, she turned around and said, "Oh yea, and we're going to go look for your new car this week too. But I want to pay for a good portion of it, and Grandma also give us some money for it too. This will be your gift for all you've done for me over the years and all that you've achieved recently."

Wow, that was just about all the icing on the cake. I had now jumped to twenty-five thousand subscribers on YouTube making good money, got the scholarship for the life coaching certification program, and my follower count on my other social media platforms were increasing as well. After browsing at a couple different dealers, we finally came to one dealer, and I saw a perfect fit for me. The car had a nice body, cool color, and was a recent model. Plus, it was affordable and within our budget. So, we went to the payment desk and purchased it, Mama paid a third, I paid a third, and then we spent the last third from Grandma's input. Since I had my license for about a year now, Mama let me drive home in my brand-new car. Mama and I both got home, and Mama said that we should all go out for barbeque to celebrate.

After we got back, it was a little late, so I decided to go to bed. Mama and Julia stayed up and wished me a good night sleep. I could just tell by the look in their eyes, they were looking at me with honor, respect, and appreciation. I went to my room shut my light off and laid in my bed. I started to think how far I've come since my childhood years.

It started off with me being in my early childhood years, trying to understand the principles of life. I didn't understand why bad things would happen to people who were considered good from what the common world standard of good was. Trying to understand why God seemed like He was ignoring our prayers and cries for help when we desperately needed them. All while I was trying to make sense of the bible and believe that which I would never understand which led to the fear of me possibly never being able to truly know God. Then growing up barely having any friends and constantly being rejected and ridiculed for my many flaws. Not knowing if God even made me for a purpose which led to me thinking that God only created me to be His laughingstock. Wondering about what He created me for, how I could get to what He created me for and how I would escape the hood, not knowing if I could even land a real job. I could go on and on about all the struggles that arose over the years, but the one that had the biggest effect on me was my dad never being around and the anxiety of me being anything like him and his troubled past.

I always wondered, what was the value beyond all of what I heard numerous people speak of. But now that I made it to this point in my life, I could finally say that I had more values that were far greater than all the negative visuals that were before me. I decided to count them out. These are some of them that came to mind as I thought about my recent rise from the dirt to success:

1) My faith in God rose significantly, increasing in leaps and bounds through all of it because I persevered. I pushed through it in the hard times even when I wanted to die. All of it produced perseverance in me that I can take with me for the rest of my life and that I can teach to my kids. To break the cycle of them not having a father so they can have a present, active father in their lives. Also, to now having an ease and peace in my soul as I always grew up wondering where I stood with God. But see that, no more. It's gone. I can truly see God for who He is.

2) I brought my whole family through it. I brought them out from that nasty hood that we were living in. I say this humbly because I didn't like to indulge in any mindset that could lead to arrogance or pride. The whole time feeling incapable of doing anything to get myself out and falling into the belief that caused

anxiety about me remaining there for life and that I would end up dead somewhere. But God had other plans. The Lord Jesus saved me. I even remember thinking that only Julia had the potential to bring us out of the hood with her athletic abilities and her dreams of going pro. But it was me, the least likely, so it made me believe in myself more and see my true value. I was made to be more than some manager guy in a clique full of guys whose attitude towards me changed simply because I wanted to walk home.

3) Then, I got to see those who set themselves as my enemies like Ashley and Deon get what was coming to them. I wasn't glad that any of those things happened to them, but I was gladder having the satisfaction of knowing that God was on my side. They rose up against me making me feel low about myself but later got their punishment from GOD! Not me, and I didn't even have to speak a word or lift a finger. Thus, I knew that God was with me and that's a valuable thing not just to assume, but to know.

4) In addition, seeing how I really impacted people with my words. Helping them get free from negative mindsets, emotions, and feelings. I know because I would get comments and messages from people telling

me this. I got a rise in following on all my social media platforms which was like a community to me. A type of a family in a sense. Some haters too, but there was more for me than against me.

These were all the visuals I could think of RIGHT NOW. Although, I felt and knew that there was a lot more that I just couldn't list off in this moment because I was so overwhelmed with joy. There were so many more valuables that it was hard for me to list them all. All those things except seeing what happened to Deon and Ashley were a small fraction of the value beyond all my visuals. Not to mention the fact that I now would be having multiple streams of income coming in, from things I wanted to do, instead of things that I disliked that bought me barely enough income to help us out. Being a co-owner at a barbershop, which at my age was uncommon, on my way to becoming a certified life coach, making money from YouTube from a platform that was continually increasing day by day, to now becoming a desired motivational speaker.

Going back to me saying that I could never see myself living in the so-called American dream. I know that was all subjective, but now I can finally say that I get to live out my version of the American dream having a well-known name and having money in the bank too. At first, I thought it was impossible for me because of all my shortcomings but with God nothing is impossible.

In an overall conclusion about my life from start to now, it had its peaks and valleys or in my case very discouraging, challenging, upsetting, traumatizing and crazy visuals but I've learned that whatever the visual is despite how bad it may be, there's a value that's waiting behind it. If not multiple values beneath the surface, but you must look for it, pray for it, believe for it to manifest, and if you have all your faith in God, expect it!! With the help of Jesus, the Lord God, I at last discovered the value beyond my visuals, and can now live in it.

The Value Beyond Visuals!

To be continued....

Scriptures pertaining to the story:

Romans 8:18 For I reckon that the sufferings of this present time are not worthy to be compared with the glory which shall be revealed in us.

(When you go through tough, hard things and you just keep a pure heart towards God, you will see how worth it it really is.)

Proverbs 19:21 There are many devices in a man's heart; nevertheless the counsel of the LORD, that shall stand.

(God has a plan for you and it will come to past if you just trust Him and seek His purpose for your life.)

1 Corinthians 7:7 For I would that all men were even as I myself. But every man hath his proper gift of God, one after this manner, and another after that.

(Everybody has a gift, so make the most out of it for the Lord.)

2 Corinthians 4:17 For our light affliction, which is but for a moment, worketh for us a far more exceeding and eternal weight of glory;

(Whatever trial or test that you may be going through, just go through it. It may seem bad but it could always be worse and it won't last forever and it will bring forth your value.)

***1 Thessalonians 3:10** Night and day praying exceedingly that we might see your face, and might perfect that which is lacking in your faith?*

(Keep praying don't give up. But don't pray out of greed or anything like that, pray that God will lead you where He wants you to go.)

***Psalm 91:14** Because he hath set his love upon me, therefore will I deliver him: I will set him on high, because he hath known my name.*

(Set your love on God, focus on Him. And He will come through for you.)

Made in the USA
Monee, IL
27 March 2022